AJ smiled.

Oh, how she loved food and the effect it had on people. That was because every dish she created was infused with her passion for cooking. She watched Shane as he was enjoying a bite of cold lobster salad, and the sheer bliss on his face made her want to fall in love.

The thought unleashed a swarm of butterflies in her stomach. She'd fed plenty of people since Danny had died, but the possibility of dating, much less giving her heart away again, hadn't seemed in the realm of available options.

The sensible part of her wanted to pull back, play it safe. But the butterflies had already flown off with her heart and even the sensible part of her couldn't do a thing to stop it.

She took a deep breath against the rush.

Oh, no, this was not good.

It was absolutely wonderful.

Dear Reader,

After college, my husband and I decided to raise our family in the small town where I grew up. Even though the surrounding area has grown tremendously over the decades, so much remains steadfast and unchanged in my community: the high school, the football stadium, the farmers' market, the quaint downtown with its old cobblestones and gigantic laurel oaks stretching protective branches over those who come to shop and eat and meet.

While some people need to get away from the old and familiar, I've always taken comfort in being a thread woven into in the well-worn fabric of an established Southern community. That's where I got my idea for *Texas Wedding,* the first of three books in the Celebrations, Inc. series. When Sergeant Shane Harrison finds himself on temporary assignment in Celebration, Texas, heroine AJ Sherwood-Antonelli shows him the importance of family, friends and community.

I hope you'll enjoy Shane and AJ's story. Please be sure to look for the final two books in this series in October and November. And be sure to let me know what you think of them. You can reach me at nrobardsthompson@yahoo.com.

Warmly,

Nancy Robards Thompson

TEXAS WEDDING

NANCY ROBARDS THOMPSON

This book is dedicated to the memory of Lynn Miller Robards. You will live forever in our hearts.

ISBN-13: 978-0-373-65696-7

TEXAS WEDDING

This edition published by arrangement with Harlequin Books S.A.

For questions and comments about the quality of this book please contact us at CustomerService@Harlequin.com.

www.Harlequin.com

Printed in U.S.A.

Books by Nancy Robards Thompson

Harlequin Special Edition

†*Fortune's Unexpected Groom* #2185
***Texas Wedding* #2214

Silhouette Special Edition

Accidental Princess #1931
Accidental Cinderella #2002
**The Family They Chose* #2026
Accidental Father #2055
Accidental Heiress #2082

Harlequin NEXT

Out with the Old, In with the New
What Happens in Paris (Stays in Paris?)
Sisters
True Confessions of the Stratford Park PTA
Like Mother, Like Daughter (But in a Good Way)
"Becoming My Mother..."
Beauty Shop Tales
An Angel in Provence

*The Baby Chase
†The Fortunes of Texas: Whirlwind Romance
**Celebrations, Inc.

Other books by this author available in ebook format.

NANCY ROBARDS THOMPSON

Award-winning author Nancy Robards Thompson is a sister, wife and mother who has lived the majority of her life south of the Mason-Dixon line. As the oldest sibling, she reveled in her ability to make her brother laugh at inappropriate moments, and she soon learned she could get away with it by proclaiming "What? I wasn't doing anything." It's no wonder that upon graduating from college with a degree in journalism, she discovered that reporting "just the facts" bored her silly. Since she hung up her press pass to write novels full-time, critics have deemed her books "funny, smart and observant." She loves chocolate, champagne, cats and art (though not necessarily in that order). When she's not writing, she enjoys spending time with her family, reading, hiking and doing yoga.

Special thanks to Caroline Phipps
for educating me on the Army.

Prologue

When the tall man entered Maya's Chocolate Shop, the warm gust of wind that blew in with him—jangling the bells on the door and ruffling the ribbons on the gift baskets—seemed to sing a certain familiar name, but Maya didn't quite catch it.

She cocked her ear and listened harder…but heard nothing. *Hmm…* She thought she'd heard a whisper, but she couldn't be sure. Especially when the door clicked shut and stillness settled over the shop. All Maya could hear was the cadence of the man's boots marking time on the wooden floor as he ventured deeper into her shop.

Even so, one thing was certain—the guy's appearance in her store had stirred the *winds of love.*

There was no mistaking it, even if she couldn't readily identify his intended.

The woman would reveal herself in due time.

In addition to being a third-generation chocolatier, Maya was *un marieur,* a matchmaker. It was an avocation of sorts. Some claimed it was her obsession. But when the winds of love blew in as they had a moment ago, she couldn't help herself. It was a challenge she couldn't resist, and she wouldn't rest until she'd done everything in her power to bring "the intendeds" together.

"Bonjour!" Maya offered the handsome man her warmest greeting, which he generously returned. His was a wide toothy smile. He looked American. Or possibly Scandinavian, though Maya's bet was on the former.

"May I help you?" she asked.

"Just looking, thanks."

Oui. Américain.

Handsome as he was, he hadn't come for her. But he had turned up for a reason, Maya's instincts insisted.

The signs were subtle. Visceral. A feeling that raised the hair on the nape of her neck and tingled its way up her nerve endings, before it settled down in the pit of her stomach. A figurative "you've got mail." A metaphorical message she couldn't completely qualify, other than to know that, in the past, when the signs presented themselves in this particular fashion, they were *never* wrong.

She regarded him for a moment as he perused the shop. He looked like a soldier, though he wasn't in uniform. There was something about his close-cropped sandy hair, his bronzed skin and those broad, broad shoulders and muscular arms. Something in the way he carried himself suggested combat.

*Hmm...*Maya thought. Perhaps the combat wasn't necessarily physical. More internal...

A man at war with himself.

All the more reason she must get busy and do her job.

"I just set out some fresh truffles," Maya said. "Would you care for a sample?"

Chapter One

Sergeant Shane Harrison regarded the photograph of the pretty blonde as he sat in his car, which was parallel parked across from the storefront. His gaze zipped from the photo to the black metal numbers marking the address, and then to the lettering on the window that spelled out Celebrations, Inc., Catering Company.

Yep, this was the place.

His gaze zagged back to the photograph for one last look at the woman's enticing smile. At least the first person he'd met in Celebration, Texas, had a pretty face. He'd always been a sucker for a pretty face. The photograph had been the tipping point that had convinced him to make this personal delivery of chocolate and snapshots to a civilian.

He wasn't in the habit of playing delivery boy for strangers. However, when he'd visited Maya's Chocolate Shop as he'd passed through St. Michel on his way back to the United States from the Middle East, he'd struck up a conversation with Maya, the shop's proprietor. When she'd learned the next stop on his tour was Celebration, Texas, she'd nearly leaped over the counter in excitement.

Maya had a good friend who'd just opened a catering business in Celebration. Her name was AJ Sherwood-Antonelli—a mouthful of a name if he'd ever heard one. Maya thought it would be fun to surprise AJ with a special delivery of "celebratory chocolates," as she put it. She'd said something about a "chocolate-gram from a nice-looking soldier"—or something like that. Her words might've embarrassed him, if he'd been prone to such a weakness. But he wasn't. In the end—after several samples of Maya's sweets—it was her bribe of a box of hand-dipped truffles as payment that convinced him to bring a box to her friend.

Actually, if the truth be told, it was the photograph of the beautiful woman that persuaded him. He studied the picture again. Something about AJ's smile captured him; or maybe it was something in the way her eyes shone as she looked through the camera.

Whatever it was, that indefinable "something" made him want to know her better. Or at least meet her. He wasn't looking for anything long-term. Actually, he wasn't looking for anything. Period.

For the next six weeks, he was stationed at Fort Hood. He'd be spending most of his days in Celebration on an undesirable assignment scouting sites for an off-base MOUT school (Military Operations Urban Terrain). The assignment, known in the army as "Realtor duty," was the hell most soldiers dreaded. Once he'd secured the venue, he'd help set up the school training facility.

Six weeks of drudgery. He couldn't think of many other things he'd rather *not* do.

Centering the stack of photographs on the box of chocolates, Shane gave himself a mental shake, preempting a downward mood spiral. The assignment was *only* six weeks. Then he'd head off on a plum European assignment he'd coveted for eighteen years. In the meantime, he needed to just suck it up.

So what was another six-week tour?

It was a trade off. That's what it was. And even though getting stuck in suburban hell made him feel like doing anything but "celebrating," maybe the diversion of female company would help pass the time.

The door chime beckoned AJ from the backroom kitchen where she'd been perfecting a selection of sliders to serve at A Taste of Celebration, a food festival sponsored by the Celebration, Texas, Chamber of Commerce. The event was next weekend, and it would be the first big community-wide showcase for her new catering company. She'd done a steady stream of business over the past year and a half out of her home kitchen, but A Taste of Celebration was the first time Celebrations, Inc. would make its debut to the public as an official business with its own commercial kitchen and office space.

It was September, and even though the holidays were a couple of months away, it wasn't too early to start getting the word out about the catering company's new digs. People would start thinking about the holidays soon, and in the meantime, there would be tailgating parties and fall festivals—all sorts of catering opportunities. A Taste of Celebration had the potential to earn her some bookings.

She wiped off her hands and made her way into the reception area. Since she was the only one in the office, she kept the door locked. Not that she felt unsafe in this town where everyone knew everyone… Okay, so maybe she did have a few issues about safety. Even so, she kept the door locked because she didn't want to be surprised by someone happening in unannounced.

But surprised she was—and a little wary—when she saw the tall, good-looking stranger peering in through the glass and clutching a sack of photographs and a small box.

She was five-three, and he had a good foot on her in height. He also had close-cropped blond hair, broad shoulders and muscular arms. Quite a nice sight to behold, but the frivolity of his Adonis-like assets faded when he rapped on the glass door again and held up one of the photos.

She squinted at it, and her curiosity blossomed when she realized it was a picture of her and her friend Maya LeBlanc.

It had been taken last fall when she and her friends had gone over to St. Michel with their boarding-school buddy Margeaux Broussard to support her as she mended relations with her terminally ill father.

Hoping she didn't have flour on her face, she wiped her hands on her apron and gave a quick swipe across her cheeks before she turned the lock and opened the door. After all, a stranger in possession of a photo of her with her friend Maya surely wasn't there to cause trouble.

She opened the door a crack. "May I help you?"

"AJ Sherwood-Antonelli?"

"Yes? I'm AJ…"

"Special delivery, all the way from St. Michel." He slid the photo through the small opening in the door. She accepted it.

"Where did you get this?"

"From Maya. This is for you, too." He held out the pink and black box, which AJ immediately recognized as Maya's signature package. Her mouth watered at the thought of the confections inside.

"She said to tell you congratulations on your new business. I think there's a note in the box."

She opened the door wider and took the chocolates. "Won't you please come in?"

He stepped inside, glancing around the unfinished lobby area—all plain, plastered drywall, no furniture. Not even a desk. A self-conscious wave washed over AJ.

She'd moved in three months ago. Essentially, Celebrations, Inc. was a one-woman show financed by her own seed money, which was supplemented by monetary and in-kind investments from her friends Caroline, Pepper and Sydney. They helped her in various capacities such as prepping desserts, marketing, booking and serving. However, AJ had been so busy with the food end of the business, she hadn't had time to fix up the front of the house.

In the little bit of free time AJ had, she'd concentrated on testing new recipes and refining the company's menu. The kitchen had been the sole focus of her efforts. There hadn't been much time left for decorating the public area of the small space she was leasing.

Pepper had been after her about it. AJ was so embarrassed by the sudden realization of how stark and unfinished this first impression must be, that she made a mental note to give Pepper the green light to have her way with it.

She could already hear her friend's I-told-you-so's. And they'd be well deserved.

Standing here with this attractive man, AJ was acutely aware that if business kept growing at the current rate, having Pepper do something about the reception area would alleviate this woefully self-conscious feeling she currently had standing here with—with—

"And *who* are you?" she asked.

"Shane Harrison." He offered his hand and she accepted, giving it a quick shake.

"Nice to meet you, Shane. How do you know Maya?"

He smiled and the appeal of his crooked grin dazzled her for a moment. "I don't, really," he said. "I happened into her shop last week while I was in St. Michel, and when she learned I was coming to Celebration, Texas, well, basically she bribed me with chocolate to bring you this care package. Oh—here are the rest of the photos."

AJ accepted them. As she flipped through them one at a time, smiling at the memory of the trip to St. Michel she, Pepper and Caroline had taken a few months ago, her mind raced as she remembered Maya talking about how she fancied herself a matchmaker.

But that's not what this special delivery is about, she told herself.

AJ stole a quick, assessing glance at Shane, then returned her gaze to the photos. He was a good-looking guy, tall and tanned and solidly built with sturdy, mile-wide shoulders. *Not at all my type.* Even so, the thought sparked a heat that started in her cleavage and crawled uncontrollably up her neck, until it burned on her cheeks.

It was ridiculous. No, not only ridiculous, just plain absurd. When was the last time a great set of shoulders caused her to blush like a high school girl with a crush?

It had been a very long time.

She hated being out of control.

As she flipped through the photos one more time, she bit the insides of her cheeks hard until finally she felt her face cooling.

"Well, Mr. Harrison—" she began.

"Actually, it's Sergeant Harrison. I'm stationed over at Fort Hood for the next six weeks or so. But actually, I'm living in town for closer proximity to a project I'm heading up."

A military man.

Even though he wasn't in uniform, she could see that he fit the bill. Physically fit with shoulders so wide he could probably carry the weight of a nation…

Inwardly, she rolled her eyes at the cheesy sentiment, bringing herself back down to earth by reminding herself that shouldering the weight of a nation went hand in hand with a willingness to fight to the death for it.

She'd once loved a man who'd sworn to serve and protect. And he was dead now. The pain of that memory helped deflate the silly direction Maya's living, breathing candygram was tempting her thoughts.

"Thank you for delivering this, Sergeant Harrison, but I have to get back to work. I was just getting ready to grill some sliders."

For a split second she considered asking him in

for a taste test. Instead, she extended her hand. He gave it a perfunctory shake. Then AJ reached for the door and held it open. "Have a nice stay in Celebration. It's a lovely town."

He offered a brisk nod and turned to leave. As she watched him walk away, she had a sinking feeling this wouldn't be the last time she saw Sergeant Shane Harrison.

Her heart betrayed her and leaped at the thought.

Chapter Two

When an assignment landed Shane in a new town, one of his first orders of personal business on his first day off was to familiarize himself with the lay of the land.

Even though he didn't particularly want to be in Celebration, Texas, he'd decided to make the best of it and explore. Earlier in the week, when he'd delivered the chocolates to AJ, he'd noticed a poster in her shop's window advertising "A Taste of Celebration," a fundraiser to benefit a new pediatric wing at Celebration Memorial Hospital. The sampling of fare from local restaurants and caterers was happening today in the town square. Despite his lack of appetite for small-town living and all the ghosts it conjured, he was always up for a good burger and a beer. Getting to know Celebration through its local cuisine was the best way to face down this assignment. Well, that and possibly the best chance to raise a glass with AJ Sherwood-Antonelli.

A pretty face and a good meal.

What more did a man need?

Shane parked on a side street of a residential neighborhood about a quarter of a mile away from downtown. He unfolded all six foot four of himself out of his shiny black Ford F-150. The truck was his baby. Since his living expenses were negligible and his life was signed over to the U.S. Army, it was the one indulgence he afforded himself. The truck had been in military storage during his tour of the Middle East. It felt good to be back in the driver's seat.

As he hit the remote, locking the truck, a loud whistle split the air. "Hey, man, nice ride."

Shane turned toward the direction of the words that weren't so much a compliment as they were a mocking challenge.

Four teenage boys loitered on the corner opposite from where he'd parked. Shane hadn't noticed them until now.

"Thanks," he returned.

Something in the group's collective posture and body language made him pause, then glance in his car's window to make sure he'd put away the GPS and anything else of value.

He had.

He looked back at the group wanting them to

know he was taking a mental snapshot of them. All four were Caucasian, probably sixteen or seventeen, all medium height, but one was taller and bigger. Three had dark hair; one was blond. They all wore sloppy T-shirts. Two sported holey jeans. One boy—the tallest kid with long, dark messy hair that hung past his shoulders—wore his pants so low they rode down his butt and his boxers were visible. Another kid was wearing long denim shorts and had a tattoo of what looked like a dragon or some sort of serpent winding around his left calf.

They certainly didn't blend in, but they were probably harmless—this was Celebration, after all. Since he'd been in town, he hadn't seen such a rough-looking gang hanging out. Maybe they'd come for the food festival. He wanted to give them the benefit of the doubt, but a voice of reason made him wary. But what was he supposed to say to the sheriff? I didn't like the way the boys were whistling at my truck?

Punks.

Putting an end to the staring standoff, Shane turned and began walking toward the square, knowing he shouldn't judge. He was new in town and hated feeling conspicuous. So, he put them out of his mind.

It had been a long week on the new assignment, highlighted by meetings with construction crew chiefs and engineers who were working on the new training facility. Shane was exhausted—not from the work itself, as it wasn't very demanding physically or mentally. It was more like babysitting.

He hadn't gotten a decent night's sleep since he'd arrived. In the army, he moved around so much he usually didn't have a problem adjusting to a new place. But he wasn't adjusting well to Celebration. The desk job gave him way too much time for clock watching and restlessness. Because work wasn't occupying his mind, his thoughts had been running an endless loop of nonsense he couldn't seem to shut off.

Even as he walked away, his mind replayed the way the teenagers had stopped their horseplay and called out to him; the way his guard had gone on instant alert; the way he'd turned back to face them down and how the short, stocky kid who seemed to be their ringleader—or at least the loudest one of the bunch—had hollered across the street, "Hey, man, nice ride."

Shane bristled again and glanced back, but the kids were gone.

Training in counter terrorism—and life's hard knocks—had taught him to be fearless in the face of danger. In fact, he liked to joke that there was nothing like a brush with death to make a man feel truly alive. But tying a man like Shane to a desk gave him too much time to think. That's when he fell apart.

He smirked at the absurdity of his thought. They were just a bunch of smart alecks and he shouldn't give them the satisfaction of responding. His reaction proved he was bone tired. This outing would clear his head, reset his mind.

With temperatures in the mid-seventies, fall was already making its presence known. Even though it was still technically summer—the equinox was two weeks away—the punishing heat of summer had given way to mild days and nights that were downright cool.

Shane drew in a breath through his nose, expecting to smell a loamy scent, autumn's calling card—it was a reflex whenever he thought of his favorite time of year—but instead, he was tantalized by the aroma of A Taste of Celebration.

His stomach growled in response. The distraction—or reminder that perhaps he and this place might reach common ground through the food—helped him reframe and redirect his thinking.

So what if the job was boring? His objective was to serve out his MOUT duty and get the hell out of Dodge…or Celebration, as the case may be. What lay on the other side of construction hell was a plum European tour where he intended to exorcise the demons that had haunted him far too long.

In the meantime, he needed to get a hold of himself and calm the monkey mind that was wearing him down. "Monkey mind" was what his mother had called it way back when he'd been prone to similar restlessness as a boy, when his mind jumped from notion to notion as a monkey swings from tree branch to tree branch.

He swiped a hand over his eyes as if the gesture could scrub away the recollection. But his mother's sweet smiling face was freshly imprinted on his mind. Memories like this were landmines that he preferred to avoid. He blew out a breath and looked around for something to refocus on.

The possibility of running into AJ again. That should be enough to grab the attention of any red-blooded man, he thought as he walked. And thinking of her did make him feel marginally better.

So, with seeing her to anticipate, what the hell was wrong with him? Feeling of loss like this hadn't hit him this hard in twenty years. Maybe it was the impending anniversary.

Twenty years. Wow. It seems like yesterday.

After the explosion that had killed his family, he'd learned to shut down his thoughts when the mind apes got restless. He knew from experience if you loved too deeply you got hurt; if you dwelled on the hurt it ended up eating you alive. So, he'd become a specialist at isolating the enemy emotion, neutralizing it so that he didn't have to give it another thought.

Shane had become an expert at feeling nothing. It made him a damn good soldier. Wasn't that all that mattered, since he had nothing else to live for?

He'd been eighteen years old when he'd lost his family—his mother, father, sister and brother. Gone. In the snap of a finger, they were gone and his world was shattered beyond repair.

Why am I alive? Why did they have to die? Maybe if I hadn't stayed behind in Italy?

In the first few years, he'd asked himself these questions nearly every day, until it had gotten to the point where the what-ifs had threatened to bury him. That's when he'd to lock it all away.

Why, all of a sudden, were the ghosts he'd so carefully sequestered haunting him again?

As he continued his journey up the tree-shaded sidewalk toward the square, he glanced at the small clapboard houses that lined the walk. His mood darkened with each well-manicured lawn he passed. After several tours of the Middle East and living in government bachelor digs when he was in the States, it was no wonder this homey little town was bringing up issues. It reminded him so much of his childhood.

Fort Hood was just far enough away that it was more practical for him to stay in a rent-by-the-week efficiency. It wasn't much, but at least it was closer to the construction site than commuting from the base.

This assignment was only temporary, he reminded himself. He'd be out of here soon enough. Then came Europe. And after that...he'd wait and see what life and the U.S. Army dictated.

In the meantime, distant strains of country music and aromas of delicious food beckoned him. His stomach growled again. Starving, he inhaled deeply, trying to discern among the mélange of inviting scents if there was a grilled burger in his near future.

It smelled promising.

As Shane closed the distance between his appetite and the town's offerings, the sound of a bouncing basketball grabbed his attention. In the driveway of a two-story brick house, two boys were engaged in a game of Horse. The sound of a blaring car horn made one of them miss the basket. A mangy looking mixed-breed dog darted across the sidewalk, having narrowly dodged the honking car. Shane watched as the mutt, who seemed unfazed by his near brush with death, loped up to the boys, barking and dancing around them, licking their faces and wiggling in delight.

"Hey! You'd better put a leash on your furry friend," Shane called to the boys. They froze, ceasing their whoops and giggles, staring at him warily as if they'd just noticed him. "He almost got hit by that car."

The boys said nothing. They just stood there, the dog in between them and the stranger.

Shane didn't mean to scare them. See, that was one of the things he hated most about small towns like Celebration. Everyone knew everyone. Everyone was accounted for…part of a family or at least the fabric of the community. It was just like where he grew up.

The boys didn't answer, so he kept walking, hoping they would heed his suggestion to curb their pet. Loss hit hard when you lived in a sheltered world that fostered a false sense of immortality. By the time he reached the next driveway, the whoops of laughter and barking began again.

In the distance, he saw the town square, a park dotted with white tents. The source of the delicious aromas, he suspected. He waited for a couple of cars to pass before making his way across Main Street.

Closer to the square, the street had been blocked off with large traffic barriers to allow for free-flowing pedestrian traffic. It appeared that the entire town of 1,288 had turned out for the food fest and that everyone was here milling about.

Did the square have room for 1,289?

Shane bought his ticket and entered the fray. The first booth he came to was a restaurant called Quiche Me Quick. They offered a sampling of quiches.

Quiche?

He hesitated. But since the samples were cut into small pieces and he could take it and eat while he kept walking, he grabbed a plate and did just that.

In fact, he walked right past the next booth. Petite Four, was offering an array of bite-size cakes that were covered in shiny, pastel-colored icing and decorated to look like little presents. Too sweet for an empty stomach. The sight of them made his teeth hurt.

The third booth was even less promising. It was Deloris's Delicacies, offering what looked like fluffy pink icing that smelled like fish. As if the appearance wasn't unappealing enough, the smell nearly did him in.

Judging by the first few booths, it looked like the festival was about froufrou food; he craved something substantial. He inhaled again to make sure the delicious smell of something cooking on the grill hadn't been a sensory mirage. It was still there. It made his mouth water.

"Hi! I'm Deloris. Care to try my salmon mousse?" A petite, middle-age woman, who looked like she would be more at home in a Junior League meeting than hawking fishy fluff, held out a white plastic spoon heaped with the unappetizing stuff. "I made it myself. When I bring it to parties everyone just goes wild over it and asks me for the recipe. They always say, 'Deloris, you should go into business and sell that mousse of yours.' So I did. Here, hon, have some."

She seemed so proud. The last thing he wanted to do was hurt her feelings. He wasn't picky, but the fact that he could smell the goo from a distance made him hesitate, despite how a steady stream of people drifted by and grabbed spoons.

"You know what? I just got here and I'm making my rounds to see what looks good. I don't want to get too full too fast."

She smiled. "Well, I understand. But you come back and see me. I'll save you a bite, okay?"

He tilted his chin in what he hoped was a noncommittal gesture. "By the way, would you happen to know where I could find the Celebrations, Inc., Catering booth?"

"I don't know right off the top of my head, hon, but I'll look at the festival map and find out for you."

She placed the mousse spoon on an iced silver tray, walked to a table at the back of the tent and returned with a map of vendor locations.

"Let's see..." She traced the page with a nail that was painted the same color as her mousse. "Ah! Here we go. We're here." She tapped the paper. "You'll want to scoot right across there." She traced a path away from her booth, around the large gazebo in the center of the square—where a Country-Western band was playing and people were line dancing—to the other side of the square. "Celebrations, Inc. is in tent number 78. Right under that big old oak tree, across from where everyone's dancing. Would you like to take this with you?" She offered him the map.

"You might need it later. But thanks for your help."

She rolled the map into a cylinder. "It was my pleasure. But hey, before you go, are you looking to secure a catering company for an upcoming event? Because I know AJ and if you told her you wanted her to use my mousse, I know she'd do it."

"Actually, I'm just stopping by her booth to say hello."

"Oh. *Ooh!*" Her eyes sparkled as if Shane had confided that he was there to propose to AJ. "How long have you known our AJ?"

Another thing he hated about small towns was how good news tended to travel fast. He needed to nip this in the bud before Deloris told the entire town he and AJ were engaged.

"Actually, I don't really know her. We have a mutual friend, and I was just stopping by for a second to say hello."

"Oh." Deloris looked decidedly disappointed.

As luck would have it, three women walked up to the booth, all hugs and squeals, apparently delighted to have found Deloris and her delicacies. Shane took that opportunity to wave goodbye and make his exit.

He meandered in the general direction Deloris had outlined, past the gazebo, toward the stately oak tree, counting down the booths until he came to number 78. That's when he realized that the heavenly scent of burgers on the grill was coming from the Celebrations, Inc. tent.

Like a petite, blonde angel, AJ was setting down a tray of small burgers. Exactly what he was craving.

Maybe I should ask her to marry me right now.

Chapter Three

Fluffy clouds like white cotton candy stood out against the brilliant blue sky. What a glorious day to be outside, giving away food. All morning, AJ kept thinking she saw—of all people—that soldier who'd brought her the chocolate. Out of the corner of her eye, she'd catch a glimpse of a tall, broad-shouldered blond guy and immediately her thoughts would skitter to Shane Harrison. Each time it turned out not to be him, a vague sense of disappointment would press down on her.

It was peculiar that she kept thinking she saw him. Usually when that happened, she would end up seeing the person who'd been on her mind.

She didn't claim to be psychic or think that the false sightings were some sort of precognition; it was just uncanny how often it happened that she thought about someone and later they'd turn up. With the number of false soldier sightings she'd had today, AJ shouldn't have been surprised when she turned around to set out her ninth tray of samples and found him standing at her tent. Nonetheless her stomach did a triple gainer.

"There you are," she said.

He narrowed his eyes and cocked his head slightly to the right. "You were expecting me?"

Ugh. "Did I say that out loud?"

"You did."

She set down the tray on the table and adjusted her latex gloves and smiled at the other people who came up and grabbed the small plates of food she was offering. The festival was so busy and she'd been working at such a brisk clip her thought must have slipped out. Out loud.

Great.

Note to self. Check internal filter. Make sure it is firmly in place.

"Actually, I was speaking in generic terms," she hedged. *Oh, peachy.* If she kept this up she'd end up digging herself into a deeper hole. Heat began to creep up her neck. "I knew someone was behind me—lots of people have visited my tent today—and I—I meant to say, 'There you are.' You know…as in 'look what we have here.' This is for you."

She nudged the tray toward him. "Have some."

But he continued to squint at her for a few more beats before shifting his gaze to the proffered platter.

"Okay. So, what *do* we have here?"

"Sliders. Three kinds. I call this one the Tailgater. It's a beef patty with bacon, cheddar and caramelized onions with barbecue sauce on the side. This one's the Parisian. It has Brie, ham and sautéed mushrooms. Then there's the Antipasto. It's topped with roasted red peppers, spicy salami, provolone and a garlic-basil aioli."

As he contemplated the platter of mini burgers, it was the first time AJ had the chance to get a good, uninterrupted look at him. She drank him in, his close-cropped sandy hair, the high cheekbones and his straight, slightly too-big nose that balanced his good looks with just the right amount of brawn. He would be too pretty with a nose any smaller—especially given the particular fullness of his lips. Yes, the lips were…sexy.

He looked up and caught her staring.

"May I try one?"

"Of course."

Her gaze slid down his broad shoulders to his arms, which were tanned to gorgeous end-of-summer bronze perfection. Her focus finally found the tray of sliders.

"In fact, I'd appreciate it if you would try all three and tell me which one you like best," she said.

"I'd love to," he said. "I'm somewhat of a burger expert."

"You are?"

She grabbed a larger paper plate from the supply she'd stashed under the table and used the tongs to dish up three sliders. When he reached for the plate, she noticed his hands were rugged, but the fingernails were short and clean.

Mentally, she checked off the *clean hands* item on the list of "Man Criteria" she kept in her head. Clean hands told a lot about a guy. Soft, manicured hands would be weird, but clean with short nails were still manly and indicated good grooming. As far as she was concerned, nasty hands were a definite deal-breaker—well, it would be a deal-breaker if she were looking for something more than his opinion on her new recipes.

"Since we're getting into football season, Celebrations, Inc. is offering catered tailgate picnics. The sliders and crispy onion straws are just some of the items on the menu."

Realizing the onion straws were missing, she turned to her friends, Sydney and Pepper, who were helping her out today.

Pepper was right behind AJ with a freshly filled tray of burgers. As she placed the burger tray down, she looked appreciatively at Shane, most likely realizing that he was one of the few people in this small Dallas suburb that she didn't know. She cleared her throat. AJ had known her for so long she didn't even have to look at her friend to know she wanted an introduction.

"Pepper Merriweather, this is Shane Harrison. He knows Maya. Can you believe it?"

"Really? *Enchanté*." Always up for a bit of drama, Pepper extended her hand, not in a handshake, but palm downward and fingers dangling, as if she expected Shane to kiss her hand.

AJ suppressed a smile. Especially when Shane hesitated a moment as if unsure what to do, and finally gave her fingertips a slight squeeze. "Very nice to meet you."

"You're obviously not from St. Michel," Pepper said.

"Pepper!" AJ said. Despite having been through finishing school and having made her debut into polite society, sometimes her friend didn't realize how off-putting her words could sound.

"What?" she asked, her expression all wide-eyed innocence.

AJ gave her a look.

"What I meant, AJ, was judging by his accent, I gather that he is an American."

She turned her attention back to Shane, suddenly all smiles and Southern sweetness. "How do you know Maya?"

Shane gave her the short version of how he'd been passing through St. Michel on his way back to the States, and Maya had asked him to bring chocolate to AJ when she learned that he was stationed at Fort Hood.

"AJ, you got chocolates from Maya and you didn't share them with me?"

"Hey! What kind of burgers are you cooking up?" asked a man who had just walked up to the table.

AJ smiled at Pepper and with an almost imperceptible nod of her head, she silently asked Pepper to tend to the customer, which she did graciously.

"Hey, Syd, how are the onion straws coming along?" AJ asked.

The pretty brunette lifted the metal basket out of the deep fryer. "I have a fresh batch right here," she said, her British accent upbeat and melodic.

For most of the morning, AJ had been cooking, and Pepper and Sydney had been expediting and greeting the potential customers who stopped by. That's why AJ felt comfortable giving Shane her full attention now, while Sydney tended to the makeshift kitchen, and Pepper answered questions.

A few seconds later, Sydney gave AJ a who's-the-hunk? look as she set a basket of onion straws on the table. Again, AJ made introductions and then put a healthy heap of onion straws on Shane's plate. Sydney uttered a polite, "Very nice to meet you," and returned to frying the onion straws.

Shane tasted the Tailgater slider first. AJ watched him bite into it. She got enormous pleasure from feeding people. Rapt, she watched Shane as he chewed and swallowed.

"What do you think?" she asked, not even trying to stifle the eagerness in her voice.

He nodded. "It's delicious, but didn't you say it had barbecue sauce with it?"

"Oh. Yes, it does." She glanced at the crowded contents of the table and saw that the barbecue sauce was, indeed, missing.

AJ got the sauce and turned around to find herself staring into the ice-blue eyes of the one person she'd hoped not to see today: her grandmother, Agnes Jane Sherwood. Grandmother's steely gaze assessed AJ. Judging by the way the matriarch frowned down her aquiline nose, AJ knew her grandmother found her lacking.

No big surprise. She always had. The only thing AJ could do was shake it off.

This was the woman for whom AJ was named—her mother's feeble attempt to get back into her estranged mother's good graces after AJ's mother had eloped with Joey Antonelli. A plumber. A man Agnes had considered so far beneath her daughter that she couldn't even see that far down the social food chain. When her daughter came back married, Agnes quit speaking to her for years.

Even though her mother and grandmother were on better terms today, Agnes still liked to grouse, "What was I supposed to say? When my friends' daughters were marrying into families such as the Connecticut Collinses or the Dallas Dashwoods, *my* daughter has married into the Antonelli Plumbing Antonellis. It was mortifying."

Apparently, it had been a huge disgrace. One so

grave that even after the young bride had saddled her innocent first born with a name like Agnes Jane Sherwood-Antonelli, grandmother hadn't let AJ's mother back into her good graces.

It was no help, either, that Agnes Jane Sherwood's namesake had decided to become a chef. Cooking was a chore the hired help quietly took care of. Not something a Sherwood fretted over and certainly not something they found enjoyable. Grandmother said, "Obviously AJ has inherited her father's working-class DNA."

Today, what made matters worse was that Grandmother was the chair of A Taste of Celebration. Obviously, the chair in name only, because she seemed just as surprised to find her granddaughter part of the festival.

"Flipping burgers? Really, Agnes Jane, how could you embarrass me— How could you embarrass *yourself* like this?"

A sudden hush seemed to settle over the square as the eye of Hurricane Agnes settled under the Celebrations, Inc. tent. As ever, her grandmother's energy was harsh and commanding, a presence that seemed to vibrate. Or maybe the vibration was simply the sound of blood rushing through AJ's ears as she stood there mortified, watching Shane watch this embarrassing confrontation.

"Have you been reduced to serving fast food?" Agnes continued.

Pepper came up behind AJ and put a supportive

hand on her shoulder. Something in that kind show of I've-got-your-back loyalty made AJ snap out of her stupor.

"Grandmother, I am test-marketing options for a football season tailgating menu that *my company* is going to offer."

It was *her company.*

She hadn't asked the woman for a penny of her millions to get Celebrations, Inc. off the ground. AJ had laid a careful plan, worked hard, scrimped and saved with the intention of gathering enough seed money to open her doors.

The opening had been put on a faster track after AJ's fiancé died, naming her the beneficiary of his life insurance policy. But not until after the money sat in a savings account for a little over three years. At first, AJ couldn't fathom spending a penny of it, paralyzed by the thought that Danny was gone and money was all she had left of him. It hadn't seemed right. It hadn't seemed fair that he'd had to die, and she was left here to try and go on without him.

For three years, AJ had lived in a daze, going through life's motions—getting up, working long hours, coming home, sleeping only to get up and do it all over again. Sleep was the only place where she found peace… At night, when her head hit the pillow, she could lose herself in dreams where Danny was alive, her family accepted him and she was happy. As a result, during the waking hours, she shut down, living in her head. This didn't escape her friends.

That's when it had hit her. He would never have wanted her to sit idle. She needed to invest that money in making her career dreams come true—something Danny had been so supportive of.

After she'd done that, it was as if Danny were right there with her every step of the way.

So, even if she were "flipping burgers," she'd rather be doing that, relying on herself and her own creativity to make or break her than living on her grandmother's terms.

AJ knew it galled her grandmother that she was *that* solvent. Thanks to Danny, a man Grandmother had deemed beneath her namesake, AJ was free, and her grandmother didn't have an ounce of control over her.

Her grandmother didn't dignify the justification of AJ's burger flipping with a comment. She just stood there with an expression so sour, AJ feared the old woman would suck on her cheeks hard enough to suck herself inside out.

As AJ stifled a smile, she realized she was still holding the bowl of homemade barbecue sauce she'd promised Shane. Why did he have to witness this ugly scene?

She turned away from her grandmother to set the bowl of sauce in front of Shane. As she did, the toe of her hot pink Dr. Martens caught on an exposed tree root. As if in slow motion, she lurched forward, splattering sauce down the front of Shane's white polo shirt.

* * *

Shane knew the barbecue sauce mishap wasn't intentional, and he tried to reassure AJ of that. He wouldn't allow her to have his shirt cleaned, and she didn't deserve her grandmother making an awkward moment worse by insisting that the Taste of Celebration committee would replace the shirt.

He declined both offers.

However, it soon became clear the woman—who he was tempted to call "the old battle-ax," but refrained because she was AJ's grandmother and that would be disrespectful—was a trying piece of work. But soon he realized Agnes Sherwood would not take no for an answer. He decided to give her his address just so she would shut up and go away.

At first he was going to give her the central address at Fort Hood. But then he decided he would give the woman a full-on dose of the working-class stiff he was. "I'm staying at the Celebration Suites, off of the highway. I don't know the address off the top of my head, but it's unit 201."

Agnes sniffed and Shane swore he saw her bristle. "Are you referring to that *place* one rents by the week?"

Never before had he heard the word *place* said with such contempt. If he didn't know better, he'd think he was renting a place in Celebration's Red Light District—if there was such a place in Perfectville, U.S.A.

"Yes, ma'am that's where I live. For the moment

anyway. I'm sort of…transient." He looked her square in the eyes and smiled.

He loved messing with people who carried a superiority complex. This woman wore hers like crown jewels. For a split second, he wondered how someone like AJ could be related to Agnes Sherwood. AJ was humble and sweet, someone who wasn't too proud to serve burgers and onion rings—or to roll up her sleeves and get the work done. Agnes Sherwood, on the other hand, seemed the type who'd never gotten her hands dirty.

After all the things he'd seen in the Middle East and his years in the army, he couldn't stand it when the idle rich put themselves above others. But it wasn't his duty to reform her.

"Agnes Jane, write down his information. Apartment number, size and brand of the shirt. I will have something sent by midweek."

With that, Queen Agnes turned and left.

They were dismissed.

AJ was thankful for the way Pepper and Sydney jumped in and distracted the customers who were kind enough to focus on the food and not the scene that had just unfolded. This left AJ free to do damage control with Shane.

"I am so sorry," AJ said to Shane.

After being humiliated by her grandmother and dousing him in barbecue sauce, what else was there to say?

She wished she could blame her grandmother for unnerving her, but really, it was her own clumsy fault. She should have been more careful and watched what she was doing. Or as Grandmother would say, "her comportment had been lacking." *Again.*

Shane was only a customer, after all. Not someone who should fluster her.

"Please don't worry about it," he said. "No harm. No foul. Now, if I'd been wearing my Dallas Mavericks jersey, that would've been another matter all together."

"Lucky me. It's not game day."

"Yeah. Lucky you."

She felt her hot skin blanch, until he grinned and winked at her. Then her cheeks went all hot again.

"The stain is drying to look like a bad tie-dye job," she said.

He gazed down at the soiled area. "I haven't worn a tie-dyed shirt since I was a teenager."

"Well, there you go. Merry Christmas, a few months early. Here, let me get a pen and some paper and I'll get your information for my grandmother."

He tried to wave her off. "Let's not. Please? Just tell her I left before you could get it."

"Are you kidding me? You saw how my grandmother is. I'm not going to cross her again. So, wait right there." Playfully, she pointed at him. "That's an order."

She grabbed a pen from her purse and picked up a napkin. She turned back to him, half expecting to see him walking away, but he was still there. He *hadn't* left. He hadn't stomped off in a furious huff—as if normal people actually stomped. Of course not. Only her grandmother did things like that. The fact remained that Shane was standing there, making light of her faux pas. At that moment, something inside of her shifted.

Besides being a very good-looking man, he seemed like a *good* man. If for no other reason than that, she wanted to get to know him better.

"Here," she said, handing him the napkin and pen. "Write down your size, the brand of shirt you like—make it something expensive since Grandmother is paying. Also, write down your apartment number and your phone number. I am going to fix you dinner since I put you through all this trouble. I'll call you and we can figure out what day this week would be good."

He regarded her for a moment. Then he tore the napkin in half and handed a piece to her.

"I'll need your number then. If I'm giving you my number, you have to give me yours. Call me old-fashioned, but I think the man should be the one to call and arrange the first date."

"Date?" AJ sputtered. Did he think she was asking for his number to call and ask him out? She tried to think of a witty retort, something to put them back on level ground, but his words, "Call me old-fashioned," resonated in her head.

"What? You don't want to go out with me?" He

frowned. “Are you rejecting me? Do you have a prejudice against men who smell like barbecue sauce?”

She loved the mischievous sparkle in his hazel eyes. Those eyes—with their green and brown and amber flecks—were almost hypnotizing.

“I don’t remember you asking me for a *date.* The last I remember is my offer to cook for you. What? You don’t like my cooking?”

Shane smiled and picked up one of the Tailgater sliders. He took a bite and chewed. AJ couldn’t help herself, her gaze dropped to his lips and for a moment, she lost herself, wondering if they tasted as good as they looked.

But then he swallowed the bite, and her gaze skittered back up to meet his. Their eyes locked.

“If today is any indication of your talents, I’m fairly certain I’ll fall in love with your cooking. But why don’t we start with a first date?”

Chapter Four

Shane couldn't remember the last time he'd asked a woman out on a date. Sure, he'd enjoyed his fair share of feminine company over the years, but as far as asking someone out… It had been a long time since the traditionalist he'd claimed to be had surfaced as it had today.

The folded half napkin she'd written her number on was in his front right pocket. After he unlocked his truck and slid behind the wheel he reached in his pocket and took it out again.

The leather seats were warm, the heat penetrating through the legs of his jeans. Still, he sat there for a moment gazing at the black ink on the napkin, the numbers that would connect him to AJ.

But before that could happen, he had to get home

and get the smell of barbecue sauce off him before it became his permanent scent.

He tucked away her phone number in the car's console, turned the ignition key and the engine purred to life.

As the light turned green at the corner, he noticed that the hoodlums who were hanging out earlier were gone. However, right before Shane accelerated to get through the intersection, the same dog he'd seen loping through traffic as he walked to the square darted in front of his car.

He slammed on the brakes just in time, narrowly missing the mutt.

Did that family have a death wish for their dog? Surely, they didn't. Maybe the animal was the crafty sort that got out despite their efforts to contain him, a regular Houdini.

Or maybe he was just an animal with wanderlust who hated to be confined. He could relate to that.

Shane pulled over and got out. He couldn't just let the dog wander. No, the least he could do was see the dog home safely. Maybe the boys hadn't closed the back gate or had inadvertently let him out as they started a new game of ball. Whatever the case, Shane decided, he would hand the dog over to an adult who would look after the creature.

By the time Shane got to the sidewalk, the dog was trotting along about thirty yards ahead. Shane whistled and to his surprise, the mutt turned and sprinted back to him.

The smelly animal jumped up on Shane's legs, licking at the stain on the front of his shirt.

"Down, boy! Sit." Shane put up a knee to discourage the jumping. Surprisingly, the dog obeyed and lowered himself to his haunches, calmly panting and looking up at Shane.

"We need to get you home before you get hurt." He tested the dog's demeanor by holding out his closed hand, which the dog sniffed and then licked. Shane gave him a few strokes, and then took a hold of the mutt's collar, which, he noticed, had no tags. The good-natured animal trotted alongside Shane the entire two blocks to the house where he'd seen the boys shooting hoops. They weren't in the driveway anymore. So Shane guided the dog up the bricked path onto the porch where he rang the doorbell.

A man who looked to be in his forties opened the door.

"Excuse me, but your dog has gotten out again," Shane said. "I almost hit him. I don't want him to get hurt."

The man looked confused and shook his head. "That's not my dog. We don't have any pets. Wife's allergic."

Shane looked from the man to the dog then back again to the man. "But I saw your boys playing with him out in the driveway earlier this afternoon."

"Must be a stray," the man answered.

"Dad, who is it?" called a young voice. Seconds later, the smaller of the two boys he'd seen earlier with the dog poked his head around the doorjamb and looked at him. The boy reached out and petted the animal. The dog whined and panted appreciatively.

"Greg, don't touch that animal."

"Aww, but he's a nice dog, Dad."

"Yeah, I hear you and your brother were playing with him this afternoon. What have I told you about touching strays? They could have rabies. Now, go wash your hands."

The boy mumbled something under his breath that Shane couldn't hear, then disappeared from the doorway, leaving Shane and the dad face-to-face.

"If he's not yours, do you know who he belongs to?" Shane asked. "I hate to see him running loose out there. That won't do anyone any good."

"That's for sure. But sorry, I've never seen the mutt before. Maybe you can take him to animal control."

"I'd hate to have to do that. You know what happens to animals there."

"Wish I could help you, but…" The man shrugged again, then shut the door, leaving Shane and the dog on the porch.

"Now what are we going to do?" Shane asked the dog.

He let go of the collar to adjust his grip and was surprised when the dog didn't sprint away. Instead, the animal sat down next to him, leaning his weight possessively against Shane's leg and staring up at him with soulful brown eyes.

Since the sun would set in a couple of hours and Shane was coming up short on leads as to who the dog belonged to, there seemed to be only one option.

"You want to come home with me tonight?"

AJ didn't expect Shane to call. Not that she was a pessimist, but since he'd been so adamant about taking *her* number and being the one who called for the date, she suspected it might have been his way of letting her down easy.

She all but snorted to herself. He was the one who'd called it a date. She'd simply offered to make dinner for him as compensation for the misery she and her grandmother had put him through.

She suspected he hadn't known what he was getting himself into when he'd told Maya he would deliver the chocolates.

That's why, as she dried the last of the equipment she'd used at the festival, she was more than surprised when her phone rang just after six-thirty, and it was Shane asking about...dog shampoo?

"A stray picked me up on the way home from the food festival," he said. "It must have been because I smelled like barbecue."

He laughed and she was glad to know he really did have a good sense of humor. So many guys would have gotten bent out of shape over being splattered with sauce—especially since he hadn't really gotten to take in much of the festival before it happened.

It occurred to AJ, when applying her qualities-a-man-must-possess list to Shane, she could check off two more items: someone who didn't take himself too seriously, and someone who was compassionate but masculine. He had to be compassionate if he picked up a stray dog. And masculine…well, all it took was one look at Shane Harrison and his masculinity was as apparent as red paint on a fire hydrant.

She paused, drying her wet hands on a dish towel, waiting for a feeling of absurdity to engulf her. But it didn't. Maybe it was because he was the one who had brought up the possibility of having a date—and he had actually followed through on calling. In the same night, no less—even if it was to ask about dog shampoo. Actually, because of this, she didn't feel quite as ridiculous dusting off the list and checking off items.

"Any idea if it's safe to use people shampoo on a dog?" Shane asked. Judging by the noises coming from his end of the line, it sounded as if he were on a headset, like he was calling her as he drove.

Teetering on the edge of uncertainty—and it wasn't just the shampoo question that made her hesitate—she smiled at the sound of his voice.

"I'm not sure, but I can look it up on my smartphone. Hold on a second."

For the first time in a long time she, she was attracted to someone. It had been *such* a long time—

since Danny had been killed. And it felt good for the butterflies to be back.

She waited for the old, familiar guilt to wash over her. Guilt that Danny was dead and she was here, lusting after another man.

No. Stop it.

It had been nearly five years since her fiancé had been killed in the line of duty.

He went to work one day and didn't come home. He was gone. Just like that.

"I guess I could have done the same thing," he said. "So if you're in the middle of something, don't worry about it."

AJ shook away the thought, refusing to let the unchangeable past stand in the way of possibility. Danny would want her to start living again. Thirty-three was too young to put herself on a shelf.

"Don't be ridiculous," she said. "I've been home for about an hour. I was just thinking about fixing myself some dinner. So let me look it up. You definitely shouldn't web surf and drive."

"I wouldn't web surf and drive," he said. "I'd pull over if I were going to do that."

"At the rate you're going, it'll be midnight before you get home. Hold on, it'll only take me a few seconds to search. But I'll have the phone away from my ear while I'm investigating."

"Okay, thanks," he said. "I appreciate your help."

She found a legitimate-looking article written by a veterinarian. "Nope. It says here that the pH of dog shampoo is two points different than people shampoo. Supposedly, that's a huge difference. It says here, using products made for people can dry out a dog's skin and cause all sorts of problems."

"Well, that's not what I wanted to hear. I guess that means I'll have to stop by the store before I get back to the apartment. He's so flea-infested, I may have to set off a bug bomb in my car. I don't want to bring him in the house without bathing him first."

"No bug bombs," said AJ. "Use borax. I don't want you to asphyxiate yourself. Do you have access to an outside hose at the apartment?"

"It's a rent-by-the-week joint. There's not even a pool I could throw him in, much less a spigot and hose for the renters' convenience."

"Bring him over to my house." AJ's stomach lurched at the boldness of her suggestion. But she would get to see him again. "We can wash him outside. And don't worry. This is not a date. I'm just trying to save you from flea infestation."

He made a sound that echoed with refusal. "I can't bring this dirty animal and all his bugs over to you. You'll never forgive me if you get an infestation."

"Borax. I'm telling you, it's good stuff. Bring him over. You can wash him in the driveway and let him dry on the back porch. He won't even have to come in the house."

By the time Shane stopped to pick up flea shampoo, dog food and a leash, it was after seven-thirty when he pulled into AJ's driveway. Her house was a modest bungalow, perched atop a small hill about five miles from downtown. From the curb, the white clapboard structure with forest-green shutters looked typical for Celebration, but he had a feeling the place AJ called home would be far from *typical*.

He walked around to the passenger side of his car, opened the door and hooked the new leash to the dog's collar. As free-spirited as the animal had seemed wandering downtown footloose and fancy-free, he was remarkably tame, sitting on the jacket Shane had spread over the front seat to protect the leather seat from the dog's overgrown toenails. He'd have to dry-clean his jacket before he could wear it again because it probably reeked of dirty dog—the same way his car smelled right now.

As he gave the mutt a few strokes, it struck him that except for being filthy and hungry, the mutt was in relatively good shape. Plus, he was wearing a collar—even if it was missing its tags. Shane frowned. Somewhere out there a family was missing a dog. Either that or the animal had been dumped.

"Do you belong to someone, buddy?"

The dog whined in response, looking up at Shane with adoring chocolate eyes.

"Come on, let's get you cleaned up."

They rang the doorbell and AJ answered a moment later, stepping outside.

"Hey," she said. She'd changed out of her chef's coat and was wearing a red T-shirt that hugged her curves in all the right places and jean shorts that made the most of her tanned legs.

"Hi." She looked way too good for washing a dog. Though he didn't really expect her to roll up her sleeves and dive in. "Thanks for letting us come over."

Her gaze dropped to the area of his stomach. Suddenly, he realized he was still wearing the same stained shirt from earlier that day. In all the commotion with the dog, he'd forgotten. He should've gone home and changed. For that matter, he should've gone home and showered and shaved, too. Maybe bringing the dog over here wasn't such a great idea after all. He could've just whisked him into the apartment shower and taken his chances.

But a little voice inside of him reminded him that the reason he was here was because he wanted to see her again. Not very good planning, but here he was. Here they were.

"Nice shirt," she said, kneeling down in front of the dog and stroking his ears.

"Yeah, this is the best dog-washing outfit I own."

She laughed. It sounded genuine and that made him feel better.

"What's his name?" AJ asked.

"Name? He doesn't have one. He's a stray."

"Oh, you poor boy," AJ cooed to the mutt. "He needs a name. You can't just keep calling him 'dog.'"

Uh-oh. Shane leaned against the porch rail. "You

name a dog, you get attached. I can't get attached right now."

"You have something against getting attached?" Her tone was light, but her frown made him think his answer was important to her.

Weighing his words, Shane looked at her for a moment—noticing her gorgeous blue eyes and sleek blond hair. "Animals. I don't get attached to animals. I can't keep this dog. My assignment here ends in six weeks. Then I'm heading to Europe. I can't take a dog with me."

Weighty silence settled around them. Then the buzz of the cicadas sliced through the stillness, making the stagnant, humid air feel like it was vibrating. Through it all she just kept looking at him, as if what he'd said didn't make sense.

So, he tried to explain. "Taking on a dog is a huge responsibility. I can't keep him. I just...can't."

AJ stood up. "I get it." She dusted off her hands and looked him square in the eyes. "They're a commitment. Come on, let's go in the backyard and wash him."

She took the dog's leash and led the way to a gate in the white picket fence that surrounded her backyard. Walking behind her, Shane tried not to watch the way her hips swayed. Or notice how nicely her butt filled out the shorts—another treasure that was hidden by the shapeless chef's coat. He also fought the urge to explain himself, but he lost.

"When I leave there's no way I can take him with me."

Smooth. Real smooth.

He should've kept his mouth shut, the way she did when they passed through the gate into the backyard. She simply pointed toward the garden hose, which was neatly coiled around a caddy attached to the house. Shane walked over and began unraveling it.

As he worked, he felt her watching him. "So, you're telling me that because you travel so much you never get attached? To anyone or anything? You just float from port to port?"

"No, I don't float, and I don't have *ports.* That's the navy. The army has bases. But no—I mean yes. I mean it's not that I consciously decide not to get attached. It's just difficult because I'm so…"

"Transient?" She looked horrified.

He snorted, unsure of whether to laugh off her comment or take her seriously. But the fact that he could see virtual walls that had gone up around her made him believe there was a hint of truth to her question.

He had to admit she'd struck a nerve in him, too. He didn't run from commitment, as she seemed to imply. Basically, he was married to the army and it wasn't fair to anyone or anything, as the case may be, to form other attachments. Especially in a place like Celebration, where he'd only be spending six weeks.

It was best to change the subject.

"Do you have a dog?" he asked.

AJ shook her head.

"You could take him. Hey! That would work. You could name him and keep him and take care of him."

AJ shot daggers at him with those blue eyes. She held up her hands. "I work too much to take on the responsibility of a dog."

He turned on the hose. "So, you work too much to make a commitment. Because a dog *is* a commitment, right? You said so yourself."

He winked at her, trying to lighten the mood.

She made a clucking noise. "Okay. Point taken."

He watched her watching him lather up the dog.

AJ bit her bottom lip, deep in thought. "I'll make a deal with you," she said. "Let's go ahead and name him, and I'll work with you to find a home for him before you leave. Deal?"

Shane stared into her eyes. In the twilight they were the color of the Mediterranean. "Deal." He heard himself utter the word before he was fully cognizant of what he was doing. He quickly added an out.

"Although, he might belong to someone because he's in pretty good shape for a stray. I better put up flyers."

"That's not a bad idea," she said. "If you take him to the vet, they can scan him to see if his previous owner had one of those chips put in him. If so, you'll know exactly where he belongs."

"Good idea. I guess I need to take him to the vet. Have him checked out. Make sure he's had his shots."

The dog sat perfectly still as Shane lathered him. The animal almost seemed to enjoy it.

"So, what should we name him?" AJ asked.

A twinge of apprehension coursed through him. Sometimes army dogs ended up locked away in kennels when owners were deployed. That kind of treatment was almost as inhumane as abandonment. Giving the dog a name wasn't a good idea and he knew it. He gazed at AJ and realized that since he'd arrived in Celebration he was doing a lot of things that weren't a good idea.

"Houdini," he said.

"Houdini?" AJ asked. "Why that name?"

Shane gave the dog a long, thoughtful look. "When I first saw him, I was on my way to the food festival. He almost got hit by a car, but he ran up to two little boys who were outside. I thought he belonged to them. But then when I was on my way home, he was loose again and ran out in front of my car. I thought that maybe he had escaped from the boys' backyard. You know, like Houdini escaping."

"Houdini." AJ beamed at Shane. "That's perfect. Hey, Houdini. Do you like your name, boy?"

The dog barked a succinct *woof,* which had Shane and AJ laughing.

"Good choice," she said. "He likes it."

So did Shane. He liked the way she was willing to roll up her sleeves and dive into the thick of the dirty work. An inexplicable warmth spread through him as they worked together scrubbing and rinsing the hound in a comfortable, companionable silence, which was broken only by the occasional "Good dog" cooed at Houdini.

After they'd finished, AJ dried the dog with a big beach towel. Shane watched her as he coiled the hose. Even soaking wet, she was the kind of gorgeous that made it hard to take his eyes off her. He wanted to reach out and run his thumb along her cheek to see if really felt as smooth as it promised. The thought of touching her stirred a want in him so fierce it was almost paralyzing.

"Since he's wet, it might be a little chilly for him out here," she said. "Why don't you two come inside and I'll cook something for us. You must be starving."

Damn right he was starving, but his hunger wouldn't be satisfied by food. The realization threw him off guard for a moment. Despite the chemistry he felt between them, he sensed that AJ Sherwood-Antonelli was not the kind of woman who had flings. He couldn't offer anything long term. Because of this, it wasn't a good idea for him to be alone with her tonight.

Houdini trotted over to Shane, who was still kneeling by the hose caddy, and shook, flinging wet-dog spray everywhere.

"Oh, no!" AJ looked as if she were doing her best to hold back peals of laughter.

"Thank, buddy." Shane laughed, because there

was nothing else he could do, and made a show of wiping off his arms. "That was just what I needed."

AJ's gaze snared his, and she laughed, too. "Come here, Houdini, let me finish drying you off."

"Yeah, buddy, you better listen to her. Go on over there and get dried off."

As if in response—or possibly just out of pure unadulterated joy—the dog dropped down, rolled onto his back and began wriggling in the grass.

"Houdini, stop," Shane commanded, but the dog kept up his canine-worm wriggle.

"Hey!" Shane gave three sharp claps. "Stop. Now."

The dog leaped to his feet, ears back, as if realizing he'd forgotten himself.

"We'll have to take a rain check on dinner. Or should I say, *I'll* take the rain check. Because I have a sneaking suspicion if you let us in, my sidekick would take a flying leap and finishing drying off on your sofa. That would be the quickest way to wear out our welcome."

She waved him off. "Don't be ridiculous. I wouldn't have invited you in if you were anywhere close to wearing out your welcome."

She bit her bottom lip and the way she was looking up at him made it difficult for him to turn down her offer. Then Houdini gave another full-body shake.

"Thanks, but no. He has no manners, and I need to change clothes."

"I have some clothes you can change into. You can clean up while I cook."

His right brow shot up. "I don't wear your size."

She looked taken aback, her mouth opening and closing before she clarified, "They're *men's* clothes."

He didn't know why, but the thought of her keeping a spare set of men's clothes around made his chest tighten in a peculiar way he didn't understand. Then again, he didn't understand a lot of the things he'd been feeling since he'd handed her that box of chocolate his first day in Celebration.

Needing to lighten the mood, he shot her a flirtatious grin. "Why do you keep a spare set of men's clothing around? Is it for the random dog washer who happens by? Or is it for when you serve barbecue?"

She smiled, but it didn't reach her eyes and he worried his teasing had struck a nerve.

"It's a long story," she said. "Not one to get into now."

A breeze rustled the tree branches, and a wind chime danced somewhere in another part of the yard.

Men's clothes. With a long story attached.

He thought back to the last time he'd had women's clothing in his house and his thoughts strayed to Italy—a dress draped over a chair back, underwear littering the floor. But questions rooted very much in the present jerked his attention back to Celebration.

Whose clothes were in AJ's house? A brother's? Her father's?

Probably not. Though if they belonged to a lover she wouldn't have asked him to stay for dinner.

He shifted his weight from one foot to another, trying to ignore a sudden burst of agitation he felt while wondering whose clothes they were. Good question: Why *did* he care?

He looked into her sea-blue eyes searching for an answer, and he thought he glimpsed a flicker of pain that seemed to match his own. A hint that they were two damaged souls who were awfully good at going about their day-to-day business pretending everything was fine. Now wasn't the time to ask about the ghosts that haunted her, but tomorrow was another day.

"You've already gone above and beyond by helping me with Houdini tonight. You've been on your feet all day. The last thing you need is to spend any more time in the kitchen. But if you're free tomorrow night, I'd love to take you out. On that date we talked about earlier today."

Chapter Five

Sunday was AJ's favorite day of the week. In the year and a half since she'd opened her catering business, only a handful of events had fallen on a Sunday. Since the rest of her days were booked with events or spent planning for them, she'd come to look forward to Sundays as her one day of rest and relaxation.

Usually, the day flew by, but since she had a date with Shane that night, this particular Sunday was creeping by at the speed of an escargot on a cold Provencal street.

She was so happy when her girlfriends Caroline, Pepper and Sydney had agreed to come over and keep her company.

AJ was making a brunch featuring an asparagus and goat cheese frittata paired with an endive salad topped with fresh pears and candied walnuts. Caroline had brought over an apple coffee cake with crumble topping and brown sugar glaze. It was a recipe she was in the process of perfecting.

By trade, Caroline was a financial analyst, but at heart, she was a frustrated baker. Ever since she'd gotten her first Easy-Bake oven in elementary school, she'd always been trying out her delicious confections on her friends. AJ was sure this cake, too, would be heaven on a plate.

And of course, what girlfriend brunch would be complete without the never-ending pitcher of Bellinis? The peach nectar and prosecco cocktail had become the foursome's signature drink.

Today AJ was nursing hers. She didn't want to be loopy or foggy when Shane arrived…in approximately seven hours and twenty-five minutes. Yes, she was counting.

In the meantime, the cooking kept her occupied. The friends, who sat on stools around AJ's kitchen island, nourished her soul.

"Pepper, what's going on at Texas Star?" asked Sydney.

"I have no idea." Pepper raised her Bellini to her lips, but paused before she sipped. "You're the one who works there, Syd, in public relations no less. You should be telling us."

Sydney looked dejected. "Right. One would think so. But there's a weird vibe. So, I was wondering if your father had said anything. You know, dinner-table talk?"

Pepper set down her glass on the granite surface of the island. The kitchen island was one of AJ's favorite things about the house. She'd redone the kitchen shortly after moving into the bungalow four years ago. About a year after Danny had been shot in the line of duty.

As feelings of loss threatened to settle around her, she shook away the thought and refocused. Yes, the center island was one of her favorite features. It allowed people to gather in the kitchen while she cooked. That way she could still be part of the party while she prepared the food.

The best of both worlds. She drew in a sharp breath. Even if Danny had been ripped out of her world.

"You do remember that I have my own place?" Pepper chided. "I can't remember the last time I sat down to dinner with my father. For that matter, I imagine my mother would say the same thing. All my father does is work. He is *never* home. But, Syd, you look really worried. What's going on?"

Sydney shrugged. "I can't say it's bad. It's just—" she shrugged again "—it's just a feeling. Something is off."

"Mom said Dad just ordered a new corporate jet," Pepper offered. "So, things must not be *too* bad. I can call him and ask if you want."

Sydney, who had just taken a sip of her Bellini, shook her head so vehemently one might have thought Pepper had offered to help her embezzle funds.

"I think maybe she's concerned about your dad knowing she's asking," said Caroline, who was sitting at the island peeling the tough parts off the asparagus.

"Give me some credit," Pepper protested. "It's not like I'd tell him I was asking for her." She pursed her lips. "I think it may be time for a lunch date with Daddy. I'll find out what you need to know."

"While you're at it, you might want to ask them when they're going to pay the catering bill I submitted," AJ said as she cracked eggs into a bowl.

"Really?" Pepper's eyes widened. "You haven't been paid? How long ago was that? Like three months?"

AJ nodded.

"Hmm..." Pepper frowned. "You might want to resubmit the invoice. Maybe it got lost in the shuffle."

It was a plausible excuse, but AJ could tell by Pepper's expression she was worried something might really be amiss.

The conversation drifted to other matters: the latest episode of a TV show to which they all were addicted; Pepper's new Christian Louboutin pumps; the red-velvet cake recipe Caroline had just perfected and would be baking for the women's club scholarship dinner that Celebrations, Inc. would cater soon;

and a new dark-chocolate mousse cupcake conquest she was determined to tame….

Even though AJ was listening, she found herself drifting inward. It was crazy that she was so nervous about her date with Shane. It was just a dinner. He would pick her up, they'd have conversation, they'd eat and he'd bring her home.

That was all. Nothing else.

Well, except for the chemistry that zinged back and forth between them. It was that chemistry that had urged her to offer Shane Danny's clothes last night.

That's what had unnerved her this morning as she contemplated seeing Shane again tonight.

Danny had been gone close to five years. Yet his clothes were still with her. When she moved from the condo, she'd packed them and had planned on donating them, but somehow the boxes had found their way into her new closet and had taken up permanent residence. She hadn't been able to give them to someone who could use them.

Until last night, when she was prepared to give Danny's clothes to Shane so he could stay a little longer. Somehow, in the light of day, the offer felt wrong. The first thing she'd thought this morning when she'd awakened was that she was glad he hadn't come in.

It would have been surreal seeing another man in her dead fiancé's clothes. The thought made her shudder.

"AJ, did you hear me?"

She looked up at the sound of her name. Caroline was staring at her, pointing with the knife to the asparagus that lay in a neat, green row on the cutting board.

"I'm sorry, what did you say?"

"I asked if you wanted me to cut them up," she repeated.

"No, just leave them whole. I'll need to blanch them before I chop them. But thanks for prepping them for me."

"We were also talking about going to a movie," Caroline said.

"Where in the world did you slip off to?" Pepper asked. "You've missed the entire conversation."

Suddenly all gazes were fixed on AJ.

"I have a lot on my mind." She busied herself whisking half-and-half into the beaten eggs.

"You've been working too much. All the more reason you should come out with us tonight. We could all go grab a bite and then see the new Johnny Depp movie. We'll have a girls' night out. How long has it been since we've spent the entire day together?"

Her friends nodded at each other and murmured guesses at how long it had been.

"I can't go because I have a date." She spat the words all at once. If she didn't tell her friends about her plans with Shane right now she might even chicken out on the date. She already had cold feet.

The way they were gaping at her certainly didn't help matters.

Pepper put her fists on her hips. Her cheeks were flushed light pink. "You mean to tell me we've been sitting here for how long—" she made a show of glancing at her Rolex, then put her fist back on her hip "—and you haven't said a word until now about this *date?*"

Caroline held up a hand to quiet Pepper, while keeping her full attention focused on AJ. "Honey, this is your first date since..." Her words trailed off as her brilliant green eyes glistened with tears.

All AJ could do was nod.

"Is it with that gorgeous guy who came to see you at the tasting yesterday?" Sydney leaned in, captivated.

Again, AJ nodded.

"I just...I...I don't know if I remember how to do this," AJ confided. "It seems like I lost Danny just yesterday, but I know it's been way too long for me to keep sitting out. It's time."

Determined to find Houdini's owners, Shane spent Sunday morning producing and printing "missing dog" flyers. He'd taken a photo of the mutt with the camera on his smartphone and emailed it to the local copy store. Within an hour, he was armed with a stack of circulars and was ready to paper Celebration.

He decided to start downtown, close to where he'd

found the dog, and work his way outward. By eleven o'clock, he and Houdini found themselves back on the street where they'd met. With the dog on a leash, Shane used a roll of packing tape he'd purchased at the copy store to hang the fliers.

"You're going to have to fight off the babes after we plaster your mug all over town."

Sitting patiently while Shane worked, the dog looked up at him and gave a good-natured bark. Shane reached down and scratched behind the animal's ears. "You're a good dog, Houdini. I'll bet your family will be glad to get you back."

Shane and the dog made their way down the street, posting fliers on every telephone pole they passed. When they got to the house where the boys had been playing basketball in the driveway, he noticed a sheriff's car there. The man who had answered the door was talking to two uniformed officers. All three of them turned and looked at Shane as he approached.

"May we have a word with you?" The two cops and the homeowner encircled him. "What are you up to this morning?"

"I found this dog yesterday. I was posting notices in an effort to find his owner." Shane held up one of the fliers.

The cops regarded him dubiously.

"May I see some identification please?" asked the heavier of the two, the one who was doing all the talking.

Shane stuck the flyers under his arm, reached

into his back pocket and pulled out his wallet. He offered his driver's license and his military ID. The cop who had been silent snatched them out of Shane's hand and walked over to the patrol car, presumably to check him out.

That was fine. He would expect no less in this close-knit community.

"Is there a problem?" Shane asked.

"Attempted burglary. Homeowner scared the perps away," the talkative cop offered coolly.

Shane shot an alarmed glance at the homeowner. "I'm sorry to hear that. Are your boys okay?"

The cop butted in. "How do you know the boys?"

Shane frowned, not liking what the deputy seemed to be implying. "I *don't* know the boys. I saw them playing basketball in the driveway yesterday when I was on my way to the food festival."

The cop nodded as he scribbled notes on a small, spiral-bound pad. Some of the neighbors had come outside and were clustered in a knot at the foot of a driveway across the street.

"What time was this?" the cop demanded.

"I don't know." Shane shrugged. "Around three o'clock?"

"And later you knocked on the door?" The deputy gestured toward the house.

"Yes." Shane adjusted his grip on Houdini's leash. "The dog ran out in front of my car. I thought he belonged to this family. So, I tried to return him."

"What made you think the dog was theirs?"

As Shane explained that he'd seen the dog run up to the boys, the cop who had been checking his ID gave the all-clear.

"He checks out." He returned Shane's ID.

Evidently not satisfied with the all-clear, the cop who had been interrogating him continued to grill him, this time about what he was doing off base. Though he seemed satisfied with Shane's answer about overseeing the construction site, he had to ask the all-important question: "What did you do last night after you left the food festival?"

"I was with a friend, AJ Sherwood-Antonelli."

After a beat of surprise, the mood changed instantly. The homeowner, who had been hovering at a safe distance, spoke for the first time, joining the cops in a chorus of, "You know AJ?"

"You're a friend of AJ's?" The cop sounded as if he wanted to believe Shane but wasn't quite ready to. "And she would corroborate this?"

"Am I being formally investigated? Because if so, I need to call my commanding officer."

The cop shut his notebook. "Oh, no. No. This is just routine. Well, it would be if we handled this sort of thing very often. We've never had a problem with crime in this community until recently. We've had a couple of incidents. You're new to town. I hope you understand that we had to cover all the angles. No offense."

Apparently, Celebration wasn't the quiet little hamlet it appeared to be.

"Plus," the officer who had been mostly silent chimed in, "from the looks of things, we believe there was more than one perpetrator."

Shane's mind shot back to the hoodlums who'd been loitering when he parked. "This might not be relevant, but yesterday, a group of four teenage boys were hanging out on the northwest corner of Main and Robinson."

Shane gave a description and told the deputy how the boys had commented on his truck. "When I saw them, they weren't doing anything wrong. But it's worth mentioning because of the timing of the break-in."

The cop squinted at his notebook and ran a hand over the razor stubble on his chin. "Yeah, you're not the only one who's seen them. Sounds like a bunch of wise guys."

After the deputies had finished taking his statement and had dismissed him, Shane turned to leave.

"So, how do you know, AJ?" The homeowner, who was sporting a completely different demeanor than a few minutes ago, suddenly stuck out his hand. "Shane, is it? I'm Bob Germaine. Sorry I didn't introduce myself last night, but you know how it is when a stranger comes to the door. Can't be too careful. Especially when you have kids."

Five minutes later, Shane found himself in Bob Germaine's kitchen, sipping a cold glass of sweet tea. The boys played with the dog out in the backyard.

"AJ's a great girl. The entire town was happy when she moved back. How do you know her?"

The earlier suspicion was replaced with genuine interest. Since Shane knew AJ, he was no longer the outsider. Because of this, he decided to couch his words carefully. "We were introduced by a mutual friend."

Bob nodded. "I've known AJ since grade school. Then her grandmother shipped her off to that fancy boarding school somewhere up north. Agnes Sherwood is a real piece of work. But I wouldn't say that too loudly. She's also a pillar of this community and a lot of people respect her. My best advice is don't cross her."

AJ was glad Shane wanted to keep things casual for their first date. She wasn't surprised. He didn't seem like a formal kind of guy. That was one of the many things she found so attractive about him.

She was a jeans-and-sweater kind of gal herself. So, that's what she'd donned for their night out—deep-blue skinny jeans, paired with her black cashmere J.Crew sweater. She pulled her blond hair back neatly into a low ponytail, applied powder, blush, mascara and lip gloss and was ready to go.

Shane knocked on her door at seven o'clock sharp, looking great in jeans and a navy button-down. The color brought out the deep blue of his eyes.

"Hi." Shane gave her a once-over and smiled. "You look great."

She stared at him...a few beats too long. She ducked her head and smiled. Why was she so nervous? "Thanks. Just let me set the alarm and I'll be right out."

"Alarm?"

"Yes, my security system," she said. "You know... single woman living alone. Can't be too careful these days."

AJ suggested they walk the half mile from her house to downtown. It was a gorgeous night. The sun was setting in the September sky, painting an abstract still life of peaches and blueberries on a pink lemonade canvas. The cicadas were out in force, serenading them with their staccato song.

Soon enough they were downtown, sitting in a window booth in Taco's Tex-Mex, sipping margaritas and making small talk over the strains of a mariachi band that was strolling throughout the restaurant.

"Have you gotten any calls about Houdini?" AJ asked.

Shane shook his head. "Not a single one."

"Oh, what a shame." AJ sipped her drink, enjoying the tang of the lime mixed with the sharpness of the salt that rimmed the glass. "What did you do with him tonight?"

"He's at home in the apartment. It's not a very big place. There's not a lot for him to get into."

AJ quirked a brow. "It was brave of you to leave him home alone."

"He did fine last night when I was sleeping. He

made himself at home right at the foot of the bed. He's housebroken and relatively calm. Obviously used to living inside."

"Which means," AJ interjected, "he probably belongs to someone who misses him desperately."

Shane was just about to sip his drink, but he stopped and gazed at her over the top of the glass. "Which is precisely why I spent the morning hanging up flyers." He winked at her and clinked his glass to hers. "Oh, and by the way, while I was out today, I met a friend of yours. Bob Germaine?"

"Oh, Bob! Right. We've known each other since elementary school."

Shane nodded. "That's what he said. Great guy. He mentioned that you left Celebration and went away to boarding school for high school?"

Oh, that. Why would Bob tell him that?

AJ toyed with the spoon at her place setting, contemplating how much she should share with Shane. Not that it was a big secret, but she simply didn't want to unload the Sherwood-Antonelli family saga on him. It was like opening Pandora's box, only in reverse. It sucked people in, and they had a hard time getting out.

However, since he'd already had a taste of the formidable Agnes Sherwood, AJ decided to give him the condensed version.

"When I turned fourteen, my grandmother decided it was time for me to receive a *proper* education." She put a snooty-sounding emphasis on *proper.* "She shipped me off to the Le Claire Academy boarding school up north. That's where she, my mother and all my sisters went. I guess you'd call Le Claire a Sherwood rite of passage. Or maybe it's more of a mandate, because my sisters and I never had a choice. It was already predestined."

Ugh. She was sounding bitter. That certainly wasn't very attractive.

"The upside was that two of my friends ended up there, too. Pepper, who you met today, and my friend Caroline, who's a financial analyst. So, I suppose if I put it into perspective, it really it wasn't so bad. I don't mean to sound like the poor little privileged girl."

He was watching her and she couldn't quite read his expression. She had an urge to fill the uncomfortable silence that seemed to echo with her words.

Should she explain to him that she'd been making her own way since graduating from high school? That she'd opted out of her grandmother's plan that mandated she attend an Ivy League college? AJ had chosen culinary school instead. For that, her grandmother still hadn't forgiven her.

Maintaining eye contact, she and Shane reached for a chip at the same time. Their hands brushed. AJ flinched and withdrew her hand, immediately feeling ridiculous.

"Please, go ahead." Shane gestured to the chips. AJ glanced up at him, but quickly let her gaze fall back to the dish of salsa. Her nerves seemed to be getting the best of her. That's what was wrong.

It had been a long time since she'd been out with a man who wasn't Danny. It had been even longer since she'd felt chemistry with a man who wasn't her late fiancé. Especially chemistry strong enough to make her jerk her hand away.

Her heart twisted in protest to the answer that came to mind: it was time she got off the shelf on which she'd placed herself, started living. In one beat her heart seemed to say, "You love Danny. Being here with a virtual stranger isn't right." The thought made her squirm inwardly, but she couldn't ignore another feeling running counter to the emotions that had formed the core of her very being for such a long time: it was time to break free and start living again.

She glanced back up at Shane, at his rugged, tanned face and those blue, blue eyes… What color blue were they…? A shade deeper than the summer sky. Definitely more blue than gray…with flecks of white and a darker blue rimming the iris. More like stormy heavens, she decided, and much more hypnotic than she cared to admit. In fact, his gaze was so intense, it almost hurt to look into his eyes—though that certainly didn't stop her.

He was a good-looking guy and she was attracted to him. No wonder this situation felt so dangerous.

There. She'd admitted it to herself: she was attracted to him. She had been from the minute he'd set foot in her shop last week. As if mocking her acknowledgment of desire, a rogue heat burned in her, starting in her heart and blazing upward.

"Just a *Sherwood* rite of passage?" he asked, breaking the spell.

"What?"

"You said boarding school was a Sherwood rite of passage. Where does the Antonelli half fit in?"

She blinked, searching for her bearings. Two servers with full trays balanced precariously on their fingertips sidestepped each other as they rushed to deliver food to opposite ends of the packed restaurant. In the distance the mariachi band sang a jubilant tune.

"As far as my grandmother is concerned, the Antonellis have never fit in. After my mom married my father she and my grandmother had a love-hate relationship. More love on my mom's part than on my grandmother's. It's a long story. Believe me. I'll save the rest for another time."

He slanted her a flirtatious glance. "So, does that mean there will be a second date?"

AJ's skin prickled at the thought. Despite the fact that he would be leaving soon, she wanted to see him again, to get to know him better, on a deeper level.

"I don't know," she answered, hoping she looked braver than she felt. "Does that mean you're going to ask me out again?"

He chuckled, a low, pleasant rumbling sound. "Of course I am."

She smiled and drew in a long breath as she savored the possibility in his words. The spice of cumin, chili and cilantro, mingled with the scent of lime and fresh, hot corn tortillas, perfuming the air. She picked out each of the fragrances as she contemplated how to steer the conversation away from her dysfunctional family without killing the mood.

"It's your turn to tell me something significant about you," she said.

"Like what?"

"I don't know…like what's your favorite sport?"

"Oh, that's easy. Basketball."

"Me, too."

His eyes lit up. "Really? To play or watch?"

"Both."

"You play? Seriously?"

"Well, not NBA-caliber, but I've been known to shred some hoops."

"That sounds like a challenge," he said. "When can we play?"

"Whenever you want. There's a court in the park."

"How about tomorrow evening?" he asked.

"Wish I could, but I have to work. I have a big job for the Celebration Women's Club. Their annual scholarship dinner."

He nodded. She didn't elaborate because she'd already monopolized enough of the conversation.

"The evening after next? You know I'm just going to keep going through the calendar until I find a night you're free. Remember, I'm new to town and other than work, I don't have anything on the books."

"So, other than Houdini, I'm your only friend?"

He smiled. "That sounds pretty pathetic, doesn't it?"

"Yeah, I guess we need to get you out more, introduce you around so you can meet some people."

Truth be told, it warmed her from the inside out knowing he wanted to spend time with her. She loved his smile, the light in his blue eyes and the way he didn't take himself too seriously. There was a nice, easy flow between them. She wanted to keep things light.

"Okay, so, I have a question for you," she said. "If you're in the army, how come I've never seen you in uniform?"

Shane glanced down at his polo as if confirming the fact. "When we're off duty we can wear civilian clothes. We're not relegated to always wearing ACUs. Only when we're on the clock."

"ACUs?"

"Army combat uniform."

"*Combat* uniforms? Even when you're not in a war zone?"

He nodded.

As ridiculous as it sounded, she hadn't really given much thought to the fact that since Shane was in the army it might mean his job was dangerous. He could go to war. The thought was sobering.

She hadn't put two and two together because he was on assignment in Celebration, the farthest place from a combat zone a soldier could get, and the three times she'd seen him, he hadn't been wearing his army fatigues.

He shrugged as if it were no big deal. "ACU is a standard-issue uniform, that's all. The army doesn't provide an outfit for every occasion. You'll have to stop by the jobsite and I'll model it for you." He grinned and shot her a mischievous wink that was just this side of cocky.

But it wasn't cocky. It was fabulous. Her skin tingled at the realization.

The ability to not take himself too seriously, of course stemmed from self-confidence. But his brand of confidence didn't cross the line into arrogance. That was one of the traits that topped her list of attractive man qualities. Yep, it was right up there with a set of mile-wide shoulders, muscular arms and sparkling blue eyes.

Shane Harrison had all four.

Taking it one step further, AJ would be willing to wager that he had six-pack abs that would make her mouth water.

Dreams of what might be hidden under that navy polo eclipsed dark thoughts of how she'd already lost one man to a dangerous job, that the last thing she needed was to fall for a soldier who might be shipped off to war and never come back.

But Shane was right here right now, very much alive. She realized there wasn't any place else she'd rather be.

Yes, Monty Hall, she just might be willing to

make a deal and risk guaranteed safety to find out if there was a sexy prize hidden behind curtain number one.

AJ blinked. To her embarrassment, she realized he'd just spoken and she hadn't heard a word he'd said.

"Did you hear about it?" Shane asked, probably repeating the words.

"I'm sorry, what did you say?" she asked, a little sheepishly.

He smiled. "You were obviously deep in thought. Where did you go?"

The mariachi band had started making its way toward their table. AJ grabbed the convenient excuse. "I'm sorry." She pointed to her ear and shook her head. "I can't hear you above the music."

Shane leaned in. So did she. Their foreheads were inches apart. The intensity of his unswerving gaze made her stomach flutter. Reflexively, her gaze dropped to his lips.

What would he taste like?

"I asked if you'd heard about the attempted break-in at Bob's house?" Shane said.

Oh. Her eyes snapped back to his. She bit her bottom lip, and even though the band was now at the table next to theirs, she leaned back a little, putting space between them.

She nodded. "Yeah, this crime wave we're having in Celebration is making everyone nervous."

AJ plucked another chip out of the basket and

scooped up some salsa. This time Shane's hands were nowhere near hers, much to her relief.

Even though there had only been a couple of break-ins, this was Celebration, Texas, a place where bad things didn't happen to good people. That's why she'd moved back after Danny was killed.

She propped her elbows on the table and rested her chin on her fists. "I guess that sounds a little melodramatic, huh?"

The band struck up strains of what AJ knew as "The Frito Bandito" song. They were singing in Spanish and she couldn't understand what they were saying aside from the "Aye-yi-yi-yi" part.

"No. I get it." Compassion deepened the blue of his eyes. "Crime is nothing to shrug off. One random act of asinine selfishness can change another person's life forever." He snapped his fingers. "Just like that."

For a split second sadness clouded his gorgeous face. Then it was gone. Still, it suggested something delicate and deep, that there was more to this man than a sexy body and stormy blue eyes in which she tended to get lost.

Since she hadn't wanted to unload her baggage on him, she sensed he was giving her the same courtesy. She'd caught a glimpse of something weighty and big in the shadow that darkened his face. She was sure the *something* was a key ingredient to who he was, something that had formed him into the person he was today. Was it a woman?

Even though she knew she shouldn't cross that line and trespass on this private ground, suddenly, she had to know.

"It sounds like you speak from experience."

He nodded. A wall went up. She saw it, palpable as if she could reach out and touch it. "Unfortunately, I think we all know someone whose life has been changed by violence."

AJ's breath caught and her thoughts snapped to Danny, and the night her own life had changed.

Just like that.

"You, too, huh?" Shane's question threw her.

Had Bob Germaine told him about Danny's death? Everyone in Celebration knew. It was the reason she'd moved back. People had talked about it for weeks. Not directly to her, of course. She'd caught the pitying glances and the tail end of whispered conversations.

Poor AJ...

Such a tragedy to happen to someone so young....

I heard the wedding invitations were addressed and ready to go into the mail....

Even as she bristled at the memories, she found herself nodding in response to Shane's question.

"My fiancé." She swallowed thickly.

"What happened?" he asked.

"He was a police officer, and he was killed."

"I'm sorry."

Something that might have been sad understanding seemed to wash over him. Empathy. But she didn't offer further explanation. She couldn't. The unspoken agreement was one piece of her puzzle in exchange for a piece of his.

It was his turn to bring something to the table.

Time seemed to stretch and extend, but finally he offered, "Do you remember hearing about the terrorist bombing—that plane that blew up over Italy—back in…? God, it's been more than twenty years now."

AJ nodded, swallowed hard. Her heart clenched as she anticipated what he was about to say.

"My family was on board—my parents, my little sister, my brother. I was supposed to be with them, but I'd stayed behind. Changed my mind at the last minute. It was summer, and I'd decided to stay in Italy…."

For a girl? The question intruded. She bit her bottom lip to keep it from slipping out. It was inappropriate because he was talking about his family. Losing his family.

"I was young and invincible—death wasn't even on my radar. Hell, I'd just turned eighteen. It was my last summer before college. I was set to conquer Europe, while I waited for my folks to come back. My dad was in the army, and they were all moving there. He was going home to get everything settled. They were supposed to be right back. Instead, they were in the wrong place at the wrong time."

He shrugged as if there was nothing else to say. She reached across the table and took his hand. Their gazes caught and lingered. Something shifted. For the first time ever, Danny's ghost surrendered to something tangible and solid.

Chapter Six

As Shane held open the restaurant door and followed AJ into the cool night, he wondered which was worse: a date laden with shallow pleasantries that led nowhere, or deep conversation that shot straight to the heart of everything he'd done his best to lock away.

Usually, when he took a woman out to dinner, the conversation skated across superficial topics. What was it about this woman that drew out the personal and private? A better question was why was he so compelled to tell her everything? It didn't make sense.

But he was beginning to realize that things didn't always have to make sense...like how he didn't want their date to end.

Taco's was a few blocks from the square, which just yesterday had been lined with white tents and filled with the food and the people of Celebration.

Was it only yesterday? It seemed like years ago.

"Mind if we take a walk before we head home? I'd like to work the edge off this dinner. I'm stuffed."

He put a hand on his stomach, feigning fullness. He'd eaten just enough, but he hadn't had enough time with AJ yet.

"Stuffed? Really? I didn't realize chile rellenos were that heavy." She quirked a disbelieving brow at him.

So, his motives were transparent. He didn't care. Especially when he saw her nod her head.

"It's a beautiful night. A walk would be nice."

He popped a breath mint into his mouth and offered her his arm. She took it. It felt natural. Together, they strolled quietly down Main Street. Rows of quaint shops lined the sidewalk—the On A Roll bakery, The Three Sisters dress shop, the Dolce Vita gourmet grocery and Barbara's beauty salon.

This was her world. All these places were familiar to her. Tonight he wanted to see her world through her eyes.

They passed an upscale restaurant with floor-to-ceiling glass doors that folded open. Customers dined alfresco at tables that edged out to the sidewalk and sported crisp white linens and small votive candles. Each table was occupied and it appeared that a small crowd was waiting for a vacancy. Soft strains of jazz and conversation drifted from the establishment, which obviously wasn't hurting for business on this pleasant Sunday might.

"Bistro Saint-Germain," Shane said, reading the restaurant's name from the French-styled wall sign. The place was more sophisticated than Taco's, but it smelled just as delicious. In a different way. "How's the food?"

"It's great," AJ said. "I worked here when I first moved back to town, before I opened the catering company."

The man who stood at the reservations stand just inside the door waved enthusiastically at AJ, then came outside to hug her. She introduced Shane to James, the owner of Bistro Saint-Germain. At once, Shane received the same genuine welcome that seemed reserved for locals only. It was a striking contrast to the cool, walls-up greetings he'd received before—if you could call those greetings. They were more aptly "I see you, stranger, and I want you to see me taking note" acknowledgments.

But tonight, with one of Celebration's own on his arm, Shane was no longer the suspiciously regarded outsider.

Tonight, he was one of them.

"Why don't you two come in for a glass of wine?" James offered. "On the house?"

"I'd love to, but we're just talking a quick walk. I have a pretty big job tomorrow night—I'm catering a dinner at the Women's Club. So I'll need to be rested and have a clear head. By the way," she added, "you're closed tomorrow, right?"

James nodded. "Why?"

"Tomorrow, I'm short three servers. They bailed on me today. I was wondering if anyone who works for you might want to pick up a little extra cash helping me out tomorrow?"

James stroked his goatee and thought a moment. "Yes, I have a couple of people I could recommend. But don't you dare think about stealing them from me, honey. You and I both know how hard it is to find good help these days."

AJ and James laughed and murmured their agreement. "I've got their numbers right here on my BlackBerry," James said. "I'll text them to you."

AJ thanked him and they said their goodbyes—a hug for her and a handshake for Shane. As they walked away from the sound of merriment, the delicious scents at their back, Shane found himself marveling…if AJ used to work here, how was it that she went from chic French cuisine to the tailgating fare he'd sampled yesterday?

Not that there was anything wrong with those sliders. On most days, given the choice, he'd take the sliders hands down over something French and fussy.

"So, what are you serving at this dinner tomorrow?" he asked.

"Why? Do you want to come?" AJ laughed.

He liked the sound of her laugh. He liked her smile and the way she tilted her head to the side when she looked up at him. “To a Women’s Club dinner? Probably not. But I might be able to help you out if you come up short on waitstaff.”

She looked at him as if his offer was the last thing she’d expected to come out of his mouth. Actually, he’d sort of surprised himself. But…yeah, he’d help her out. Why not?

“But you already have a job,” she said.

“I’m not looking for a job. But I do have evenings off.” He shoved his hands in his pockets as they walked.

“You’d want to spend your evening moonlighting for a catering company? Does the army allow that?”

She slipped her arm through his again, and the gesture warmed him. He liked the feel of her small hand on his forearm. “Maybe we could file that one under don’t ask, don’t tell. Besides I wouldn’t expect you to pay me.”

She gazed up at him and knit her brow. “Well, I certainly wouldn’t expect you to work for free.”

“Then I’ll work for food. I don’t get very many home-cooked meals. What exactly does the job require?”

“I take it you’ve never worked catering service before?”

“Is this an interview?” He smiled to let her know he was kidding.

She waved her hand as if trying to erase her words. “That came out wrong. This is *not* an interview. I didn't mean for it to sound like one. I'm sure you're a quick study."

It felt good walking so close to her, savoring the feel of her warm skin on his, the nearness of her body, the way that she swayed when she walked, which sometimes caused her upper arm to press into his. "Since I joined the army right out of high school, I haven't had any opportunities to wait tables or learn the fine art of catering."

"I see," she said. "So you've never done time at the grill before?"

He shrugged. "Heartbreaking, I know, but I guess that's life."

"Seriously, is this project you're working on in Austin typical of what you normally do for the army? Will you be based here for quite a while?"

Yesterday, they had joked about his job being transient, but that was for the benefit of her grandmother. Now, he sensed she wanted to know how much truth was there. But before he could answer her, a couple walking toward them began smiling and waving.

"AJ, so good to see you," said a petite woman with dark hair, as she pulled AJ into an exuberant hug.

"Sasha, how are you?" AJ returned. "I want you to meet Shane Harrison. He's in town working on a project for the army. Shane, this is Sasha and Patrick Green, longtime friends of mine. We all grew up right here in Celebration."

Wow, did anyone *leave* this town? Not that there

was anything wrong with staying or coming back here to live. Choosing to stay in the town in which you grew up didn't mean a person was boring or unadventurous. It made them stable and...family oriented?

In fact the majority of the people he'd met seemed the sort he'd like to share a community with, if he were looking for that sort of life. Celebration would probably be a fabulous place to settle down and raise a family. After all, even AJ had left and found her way back.

"Hi, Shane, nice to meet you," said Patrick. "How long are you in town?"

"Just until I complete the project I'm working on. Probably a bit shy of two months."

AJ's gaze shot to his. Something he couldn't identify flashed in her eyes, but she glanced away and smiled before he could read her. Even in the short time he'd known her, he'd realized she had several different types of smiles: the way she smiled at the potential customers at the food fair; the carefree smile her friends elicited; the smile she mustered when she was dealing with her grandmother. He wanted to think she even had a special smile that lit up her face when she looked at him.

Right now, the way her lips curved up at the corners matched none of the expressions he'd seen before. He wasn't sure what to make of it.

"Then where are you headed after your assignment is done?" asked Patrick.

"As it stands right now, Italy, but things can change."

"Italy! We love Italy." Sasha and Patrick *oohed* and *ahed.* "What part? We were in Venice last year."

"Vicenza, in northern Italy. There's an army base there."

He wasn't sure if they heard him, because they were exchanging a look that was reserved solely for couples who shared intimate memories and private jokes. In that moment, it seemed as if the entire world had fallen away, that he and AJ weren't standing right in front of the starry-eyed couple.

He glanced at AJ, who was still wearing her Mona Lisa smile. What had changed? Was she upset that his assignment in Celebration was only temporary? Maybe *upset* was too strong a word...but she seemed guarded, protecting herself. And that could only mean one thing: she, too, felt the chemistry that had been brewing between them tonight. At least until he'd talked about moving on to his next assignment.

He glanced at Sasha and Patrick as they resumed the conversation with AJ, shifting from their time in Italy to the here and now.

He'd never experienced what he sensed existed between this couple. He'd certainly gotten to know plenty of women. He'd been intimate with his share. Maybe even thought he'd been in love once or twice.

But he'd never had *that* with a woman.

It stirred something in him...loss? No.

Longing?

Let's not go there.

Instead, he watched AJ as she talked to her friends about everything from AJ's business to the new pottery painting shop that a former classmate of theirs was opening, to a meeting about forming a neighborhood watch program and how terrible it was that crime had found Celebration—and yes, all three of them would be attending the meeting.

As they talked, Shane glanced from AJ, to the Greens' entwined hands, to the softly lit storefronts lining Main Street, to the square a little farther down the road.

Obviously people returned to Celebration for a reason…and this sense of friendship, this sense of community was probably it. He wondered what it would be like to belong. To not be a stranger who was poised to move along even before he'd unpacked in the city in which he was arriving.

He let his mind go and imagined what it would be like to shop in these stores for food and clothing and hardware. To instinctively know where to find anything he might need and walk right to it without wandering or asking someone to point you in the right direction.

For the most part, small town living—or at least life in a town *this* small—meant your life was an open book. Shane didn't have anything to hide. So that's not what made him squirm. What did was the thought of loving again and losing everything.

Been there, done that. It could all be taken away so easily.

Celebration was not so dissimilar from Burns, Oklahoma, where he'd grown up. Was this what his life might have been like if his family hadn't died?

He clenched his fists, as if trying to tamp down the question. But it still popped up. Would he have gone away to college and come back to set down roots if he hadn't known how easily roots could be extracted by the unmerciful hand of death?

He refused to even speculate. Probably because he couldn't. His life was what it was. There was no sense in dwelling on a past that couldn't be changed.

After Shane and AJ said good-night to the Greens, they continued their stroll toward the square. Only this time something felt different. AJ didn't loop her arm through his; there was more distance between them as she said hello to several more people who were also walking through downtown tonight. But with the others, she didn't stop and chat, she didn't introduce him.

The park looked different at night with its subtle lighting and the absence of the white tents that had changed the landscape of the park yesterday. Tonight, the redbrick City Hall building, looking important and stately, was plainly visible on the west side of the square. Yesterday, it had mostly been obscured by the tents. In the center of the square, the cascading water of a large, lit fountain played a splashing symphony. He led the way to it, saying, "Let's sit down for a minute."

Wordlessly, she agreed, and took a seat next to him on the ledge.

"I've had a really nice time tonight," he said.

"I have, too."

He was trying to find the words to explain that even if he was only going to be here for a couple of months, he still wanted to see her. But every time he tried to put something together in his head, it sounded inadequate.

So he stayed silent hoping that the right words would come to him. Then as if in answer to his prayers, a streak of glittering light blazed across the sky. He leaned in so that his cheek was right next to hers and pointed at the sky.

"Look, there's a shooting star," he said. "Make a wish."

AJ wished for Shane to kiss her.

The way he'd leaned in so suddenly, she thought he would. His face was so close to hers, she found herself inhaling his air. But he didn't kiss her. Instead, he leaned back on his elbows and gazed into the clear, inky sky.

AJ stilled, reminding herself that kissing Shane was a bad idea. It had been a long time since she'd kissed a man who wasn't Danny. Since Shane was leaving to go halfway around the world after he was finished here, it was probably better that she didn't allow herself to fall for him.

Looking for something—anything—to break the silence, she heard herself say, "Shooting stars remind me of my father," she said. "As crazy as that might sound."

"It doesn't sound crazy. It's another piece to add the AJ Sherwood-Antonelli puzzle. Tell me more, so that I can keep filling in the missing pieces."

She turned to him. "No, it's your turn. I told you something, now you need to tell me something, because you, Mr. I'm-Here-for-Two-Months-then-Jetting-Off-to-Italy are just as big an enigma as you claim I am."

He glanced over at her and smiled. His teeth looked breathtakingly white and perfect in the low light.

"My turn? I didn't realize we were playing a game." The shifting glow from the fountain caught the mirth in his eyes.

"You're the one who called me a puzzle. Last time I checked, puzzles were games."

He nodded, then returned his gaze to the sky.

It was so easy to banter with him. It felt almost like a sport. Or at least a match of wits.

"So what you're saying is you'll tell me something about you, but then I have to tell you something about me? Like an even exchange?"

"You're smarter than you look."

"*Ouch!* That was harsh."

She cringed. “That came out completely wrong.”

What she meant was someone with his good looks was not usually quite so astute, but she sensed that if she tried to explain herself she’d end up digging herself in deeper.

No, much better to quit while you’re ahead—

“My family is gone.” He broke the silence. “I lost them all in an accident. So, I suppose, technically, that would make me an orphan.”

AJ stilled again. This time her heart clenched and ached for him. She wasn’t quite sure what to say. “I’m sorry” seemed so woefully inadequate.

So, she reached out and put her hand on his shoulder.

He sat up and drew her hand to his lips, kissing her knuckles. The gesture was so sweet, so tender, it startled her.

“Your turn,” he said, lacing his fingers through hers.

The intimacy—the puzzle piece he’d shared, the hand kiss, the awareness of her hand in his—it threw her off balance, messing up her equilibrium.

Dating again after all these years felt strange. She wondered whether that was what she should she tell him? Tell him he was the first man in nearly five years who had tempted her?

No. Even she knew one of the principle rules of Dating 101 was to not talk about your exes—especially not your dead fiancé. Well, not on the first date anyway. Especially when this man, who was very much alive, has somehow shifted closer and was now toying with a strand of her hair.

She could either pull away and call it a night or lean in and…stay?

"Are you okay?" he murmured.

Her skin tingled in response. A clear answer to the question of what she wanted. She nodded. He shifted closer, until his forehead rested on hers. His lips were whisper close and he moved his head so that they were cheek to cheek, his lips still a breath away from her skin.

Now, he was caressing her shoulders, and her last shreds of trepidation fell away to the feel of his touch.

Until this moment, she hadn't realized just how much she'd craved a man's touch.

Not just any man's touch.

The right man's touch.

This man's touch.

Her heart pounded. He was going to kiss her, and she wanted him to. She had no idea what would happen tomorrow or in the next hour, for that matter, but as he slipped his arms around her and pulled her closer, she gave herself over to the longing that blossomed inside of her.

His breath was minty-hot and inviting, eliciting a ragged sigh from her that escaped on a shudder.

His touch was so sure, yet heartbreakingly gentle. It felt safe and right—two things she hadn't felt in ages. Here, in his arms, was the perfect refuge where she could fall head over heels and disappear into a place where life made sense, where she didn't have to justify the choices she'd made or the person she wanted to be with.

She turned toward him ever so slightly and he turned to meet her, his lips brushing hers. The kiss started slow and soft. It was a whisper of a kiss, leisurely and slow, with brushes of lips and hints of tongue that made her heart pound and her body say *yes!* His lips tasted like heaven, and despite the vague buzz in her head, warning that she was kissing a man who was not Danny, she didn't want Shane to stop.

As if reading her mind, the gentle brushes burst into a voracious hunger that had her parting her lips to deepen the kiss. She opened her mouth, fisting her hands into his shirt, pulling their bodies even closer, clinging to him as if her next life breath would come from him and him alone. He held her tight and deepened the kiss even more.

For a moment, she disappeared into the taste of him—an exotic mix of mint, a hint of margaritas, the salsa they'd shared and something indefinable—something male that threatened to drive her over the edge.

Feelings she thought had died with Danny were bustling and blossoming into a passion that eclipsed her once-logical rationale for protecting her heart. All those reasons why not began to contract and fall away until there was nothing left except raw need and desire.

AJ had no idea how much time had passed when they finally came up for air.

She didn't know if it was because of the margaritas or the conversation or the kiss—or the synergy of the three—but she liked the rush. She hadn't felt this alive...this *free* and unencumbered by past grief and the uncertainty since—well, it had been way too long.

Tonight she was free to enjoy this exceptionally sexy, broad-shouldered man—no strings attached. That's all that mattered at the moment. The only thing she knew for sure was she wanted more.

Shane saw the flash out of the corner of his eye. It cut through the fog of delirium enveloping him as he kissed AJ. He'd seen metaphorical fireworks as they'd kissed...those sparks ignited a flame inside him, but the flare that dragged him back to reality was literal.

Reluctantly, he pulled back so he could get a better look over AJ's shoulder.

"Look." He gestured toward the south side of the park where azalea bushes grew in thick, crowded clusters.

"Oh, my God! Is something on fire?" She jumped to her feet. Shane was right beside her as they made their way toward the blaze.

"Call 911," he said.

The words were no sooner out of his mouth when he caught sight of the same hoodlum he'd seen on the street corner the day he went to the food festival. He and two other teens were running away.

Shane took hold of AJ's arm and silently directed her to stop, but by that time they were gone. "Some kids were over there. I recognize one of them."

AJ handed her cell phone to Shane. "Here, why don't you talk to the 911 operator? Tell her what you know."

Chapter Seven

She stood in the Women's Club kitchen taking inventory of the supplies she and the servers she'd hired had unloaded from the Celebrations, Inc. van. It was already five-fifteen. Guests would arrive at seven o'clock for the cocktail hour, then sit down to dinner at eight.

AJ only had an hour and forty-five minutes to pull everything together. Yet she couldn't seem to get out of her own way. Thank goodness everything was pretty well organized because she was distracted. Her mind kept replaying a loop of the unexpected kiss she and Shane had shared last night by the fountain.

The kiss and the fire.

It turned out that the kids had ignited some

gasoline-soaked rags and tossed them into a garbage can that was near an old oak tree. They'd gotten away before the police could catch them. But at least the fire had been extinguished before it got out of control.

What was this world coming to? She might not have been so shocked if it had happened in Dallas. But senseless vandalism in Celebration? It was a prank that could've been a lot worse if she and Shane hadn't been in the park.

She pressed her fingers to her lips, remembering the sensual lingering of Shane's mouth on hers, the heady taste of him—a hint of lime from the margaritas, a whisper of his after-dinner espresso, which was nearly masked by the breath mint he'd put in his mouth as they'd left the restaurant. A mélange of flavors she craved, and the last thing she should be thinking about right now as the clock ticked away the minutes until the dinner hour.

And as for the vandalism—she needed to quit dwelling on the negative—there would be plenty of discussion about that at a meeting later that week where the town would discuss organizing a neighborhood watch program. Who would've ever imagined it would come to that in sleepy Celebration? The thought made her pulse spike.

She bit her bottom lip. Shane would be there at five-thirty to help with tonight's event. For the next fifteen minutes—until he arrived—she could allow her mind to drift back to the kiss as she got herself organized.

As she daydreamed she realized the irony. To keep herself from feeling physically vulnerable, she was opening herself to emotional vulnerability.

She pressed her lips into a flat line. Maybe it was a better idea to clear her mind and focus on her to-do list. Tonight was important. It was the annual Women's Club Scholarship Awards dinner—a virtual audition for more business. AJ had to be on top of her game. These women could make or break her business. She needed to impress each and every one of them. Especially Pepper's mother, Marjory Merriweather. Not only was Marjory one of the Dallas area's foremost socialites, she was this year's president of the Women's Club and the wife of Texas Star Energy Corp founder, Harris Merriweather, the main provider of scholarships for tonight's celebration. AJ had proven herself by doing a few small catering jobs for Texas Star, but at Pepper's urging, Marjory had gone out on a limb hiring her to cater the club's biggest event of the year. There was no way AJ would let her down. That meant she needed to get her head in the game and her mind off Shane Harrison.

Centering herself, she vowed not to look at her watch or give Shane or the vandals another thought… until Shane arrived. With one last wistful glance at the door, AJ took her list from her pocket and reviewed her plan. Since her very first catering job, she'd been making to-do lists. They were her road maps. They helped to clear her mind so she could focus on the food and the guests and not worry about the logistics.

First, AJ set out her knives, a ritual that signaled the start of the job, like a gunshot at the start of a race. Then she reviewed the menu, which Marjory had personally selected: glazed Cornish hens, chestnut risotto, sautéed green beans and a salad of watercress, blue cheese, pears and walnuts.

Of course, much of the food was already prepped, but the menu still required some last minute attention before the servers could plate it.

Marjory, Harris and Pepper were like family to AJ. With that in mind, AJ approached tonight's dinner as if she were cooking for family—well, family and seventy-two of their closest friends.

Pepper was joining her parents for dinner tonight at the head table and would be able to give AJ the inside scoop. She'd also promised to do a little soft selling, even though AJ didn't put her up to it. If anyone could employ the power of suggestion and not make people feel as if they were being *sold,* it was Pepper. She was a tastemaker who had a knack for steering people to the bandwagon without making them feel that they had been shepherded.

Pepper had a talent, and AJ wanted to hire her to work her magic in the bookings department of Celebrations, Inc. However, so far, Pepper had been elusive, not wanting to formally commit. Soon, they'd have to have a serious talk about formalizing the arrangement. To build her business, AJ needed a permanent staff—or even partners—who would head up the catering company's various divisions: bookings; public relations/front-of-house manager; breads, desserts and pastries.

As if on cue, Caroline walked in with an armload of freshly baked French bread loaves. AJ tried to ignore the way her heart leaped and then plummeted when she realized it wasn't Shane entering the kitchen. Not that she wasn't happy to see her friend, but…

Caroline must have read the disappointment on AJ's face. "What's wrong?" she asked, setting the loaves on the stainless-steel prep counter. "I heard about the fire in the park last night. What is going on around here?" Before AJ could answer, Caroline had grabbed a push cart and was wheeling it toward the door. "I guess we'll figure that out at the town meeting the day after tomorrow. Are you going?"

"Of course I am," said AJ.

"Well, good. No sense in worrying about things now. I know you're on a tight schedule and I have to get back to work. The cakes are in the car. They look gorgeous, if I do say so myself. Will you help me carry them in?"

In addition to the bread, AJ had contracted Caroline to make ten coconut-dusted, red-velvet cakes for dessert. Caroline had spent months perfecting the recipe: she found just the right amount of cocoa powder—but not too much—and she tested cream cheese icing versus a vanilla-flavored concoction she whipped up on the stovetop. It produced a final product that resembled whipped cream.

They'd agreed on the latter variety for tonight's dessert—with a final dusting of coconut—because it was different. And delicious.

Shane's kiss had also been delicious....

AJ mentally shook the thought from her mind and bit her bottom lip as she followed Caroline outside to help her bring in the cakes.

"I was up until three this morning baking," Caroline said. Only then, in the golden late afternoon light, did AJ notice the weariness on her friend's face.

"Did you work today?" she asked.

"Of course I did. We're in the middle of a project and my father is on the warpath. No one is allowed to take vacation or even get sick until we close this deal."

"He makes people schedule sick days?" AJ asked, only half joking.

Caroline shrugged as she put the last white cake box on the cart and closed the hatch of her SUV. "You know my father."

Yes, AJ did. She also knew how miserable Caroline was working for him. That was all the more reason she wanted to provide an out for her friend. She was close to convincing Caroline to leave the world of high finance and join her permanently as Celebrations' pastry chef. At least she'd have a stake in a business she enjoyed—and AJ wouldn't have to outsource desserts anymore.

Caroline loved to bake and was darn good at it. However, as witnessed by the late hours she'd pulled to deliver fresh cakes for tonight's event, it was difficult for her to stay up late baking and make it to the office early with a clear head ready to crunch numbers. Leaving her day job wasn't an easy decision, either. She'd followed the family path getting a masters degree in business administration from Harvard Business School because her father had, as had his father before him and his before him and so on. If AJ had a penny for every time Caroline had confided how much she hated her job and would rather do something she enjoyed—like baking red-velvet cakes until she produced confectionery perfection—AJ would be a very wealthy woman.

Seeing the sheer exhaustion drawing on her friend's face underscored the need to have that let's-get-serious talk with her friends. AJ wrote it on her mental to-do list. Later this week, as Pepper, Caroline and Sydney toasted the success of the Women's Club scholarship dinner, they would have a serious talk.

However, before that toast of success could happen, AJ had a long night and a lot of work ahead of her.

As she and Caroline wheeled the cart toward the kitchen door, AJ heard the sound of tires crunching on gravel. Her heart lurched as she looked up and caught sight of a shiny, black Ford F-150 pickup truck pulling into the parking lot.

Shane.

As Shane steered the truck into the driveway of the banquet hall, he caught sight of AJ balancing what looked like two white cake boxes in her hands. He hadn't talked to her since last night, and only now did he realize it was a relief to see that everything appeared to be back to normal after the fire.

The fire. He resented the fact that not only were the thugs wreaking havoc on people who wanted nothing more than to live quietly in a community in which they took pride, but that this gang of hooligans had also ruined what should've been an otherwise great night.

He'd wanted to kiss AJ since the moment he met her. Never in his wildest imagination had he thought their first kiss would end like it did.

In a roundabout way, the gang that had been terrorizing Celebration had dredged up memories of Shane's own loss. The parallel was when innocent people got in way of criminals, it never ended happily. There was no way in hell Shane was going to sit back and let these misdirected hoodlums terrify this community.

As he pulled into a parking space that faced the building, his gaze snared AJ's. The calm he sensed in her stilled the outrage that had been simmering in him all day. Her eyes were as warm and blue as the

Mediterranean where Shane had swum as a kid. She waved, and the serene curve of her smile took him back to their kiss. He wanted nothing more than to pull her into his arms, tell her she was safe and kiss her until she believed it.

He jumped out of the truck's cab intending to help her carry in the boxes. That's when he noticed the woman who was pushing a cart loaded down with similar packages to the ones AJ was holding.

The other woman was dressed in a business suit—not in the all-black catering "uniform" AJ had asked Shane to wear for tonight. The woman in the suit kept on her journey toward what Shane figured must be the kitchen.

"Hey," he said, reaching for AJ's load as he approached her. "Let me help you."

"Hi. Thanks," she said, looking even prettier in her white chef's jacket in the bright of day than she had last night under the moon light in the park. "Just be very careful not to tilt them. That's tonight's dessert."

The handoff was successful, and AJ gestured to the woman pushing the cart. "Caroline baked them. Best red-velvet cake you'll ever taste."

Reflexively, his gaze dropped to AJ's lips…wanting another taste to see if they tasted even sweeter today than they had last night…but he caught himself and shifted his focus to the woman with the cart.

"I hope I get a taste," he murmured. "Of the cake."

"We try to test everything before it goes out," AJ

said. "Although I'll bet I've already eaten a whole cake's worth of test pieces as Caroline was perfecting the recipe. Oh, and by the way, Caroline, this is Shane. Shane, this is Caroline."

They exchanged greetings, and by that time, AJ was holding open the kitchen door, motioning them inside. "Just leave the cakes on the cart," she directed. "Put them right over there in the far corner where they'll be out of the way. We won't plate dessert until after the main course goes out."

Shane followed Caroline as she pushed the cart in direction that AJ had indicated. "You can put the extra boxes right there with those." She pointed to the row of boxes on the cart's top shelf. "Center them on top." He safely deposited the two cakes in his charge where she had specified.

As he turned around, he gave the kitchen the once-over, taking in the industrial space, the large, multitiered metal carts filled with food covered in plastic wrap. There were piles of vegetables on the stainless-steel counters, which a woman he'd not yet met was washing in one of the deep sinks. Someone had set out bottles of oil, cloves of garlic and spices. Cooking pots and utensils waited at the ready near something that looked like… a portable oven?

"Did you bring an oven, too?" he asked.

"Of course she did," said Caroline.

AJ shrugged. "I never know how other ovens are going to heat. I can't take a chance on the food not coming out perfectly."

He smiled. "You don't give anything up to chance do you?"

She hesitated, narrowing her eyes, as if weighing his comment. "Not when it comes to something this important."

As AJ talked to Caroline, who was getting ready to leave, he gave the kitchen another once-over, he realized AJ had indeed brought everything but the kitchen sink. He guessed she would've brought one of those, too, if she didn't trust the one available.

She seemed to trust him, and he didn't want to disappoint her or slow down what seemed to be a finely tuned schedule, choreographed down to when each plate was set before the guests.

He'd driven tanks and fired M16A2 rifles without blinking an eye, but standing in the kitchen looking at all the uncooked vegetables and various gadgets he had no idea how to use, he sensed he was out of his league.

Maybe this wasn't a good idea. But as AJ stood beside him, looking like something that could soothe his weary soul, he remembered exactly what had been on his mind when he'd volunteered to help. He surrendered control and prepared himself to start taking orders…even if that meant cooking.

"By the way, Shane," AJ said, "any word on the guys who started the fire in the park last night?"

Caroline hitched the strap of her purse higher up on her shoulder, then paused, listening.

Shane shook his head. "I talked to the sheriff

around four o'clock. No arrests yet, but they do have a solid lead they're following."

He could tell by the looks on their faces that they were hoping for a different answer. Hell, he wanted a different answer. He wanted nothing more than to hear that the teens were off the street before they hurt someone or caused any more damage.

"Are you going to the town meeting?" Caroline asked.

Shane blinked. He'd seen signs that had appeared around town today, but he hadn't thought about attending. He was, after all, temporary.

"You are coming, aren't you?" AJ asked. There was an urgency in her voice that instantly had Shane rethinking his indecision. "You've seen the guys who have been causing the trouble…twice."

"Okay…I guess I can be there." Relief illuminated both of the women's faces. "Sure, I'll come. Right after work."

"Hey, AJ." A guy who was dressed in the all-black uniform of the waitstaff joined them. "Is this the floor plan for the set up of the dining room?"

The guy held up an eleven-by-seventeen-inch piece of paper with what looked like a schematic design.

AJ nodded. "We're going to focus on the front of the house first. You all can get started on that in a minute, but first, I'd like to call everyone together for introductions and a quick meeting."

Caroline said goodbye, and AJ introduced the

team: three people she used regularly and three, including Shane, who were temporary help for tonight. AJ went over the menu, the order of events and the floor plan. She split the staff into teams and put five to work as the front-of-the-house team, moving tables and chairs into the configuration indicated on the floor plan, and then dressing and setting the tables so they would be ready for the centerpieces that, according to the schedule, would be delivered at six o'clock.

Shane and AJ were the only two on the "kitchen team," as she called it. It was nice to have a moment alone with her before all hell broke loose and service for tonight's dinner started. Shane pushed up his sleeves ready to get to work preparing the green beans to be steamed.

"It's the first step before they're sautéed in butter," AJ told him. "That's the secret. Butter…lots and lots of butter. Now you know."

She shrugged as if she'd just surrendered the code to catering success.

"Good. Now that I know your secret, I'll have a career to fall back on when I retire from the army next year." He winked at her.

She did a double take, scrunched up her nose in that way that made him smile. "Retire?"

He nodded. "Yep."

"You're not old enough to retire."

"Next year, I'll have twenty years of service in. That's enough to retire."

She blinked at him, looking a little stunned. "So, how old were you when you joined?"

"Eighteen. Right after my family's...accident."

Accident, hell. Their murder was no an accident. It was a cold, cruel and deliberate act of terrorism. He'd used the word *accident* because he didn't want to get on his soap box and spew anger all over the dinner he was helping AJ prepare for the members of the Women's Club who weren't so different from his own family. Or at least what he could remember of them. Twenty years gone and memories had shifted into soft focus. Lost loved ones were idealized. And that was perfectly fine with him. It was the least his family deserved, because they—and all the other innocent people on board that ill-fated flight—certainly didn't deserve to bear the wrath of an insane group of rebels.

"Is that why you joined?" AJ's voice was low. She set down the paring knife she had been using to cut the ends off of the beans. She touched his arm, and their gazes hung together, unwavering, hers laced with compassion.

He nodded, pressing his lips together, as if doing that might seal off the anger that still simmered inside him after all these years and longed to seep out. Once he had steadied himself, he said, "Yeah, joining up was my way of fighting back. It was either that or wage my own personal jihad. I figured I stood a better chance of keeping what happened to my family from happening to someone else by joining the Army."

"That's pretty levelheaded for a teenager," she said.

"I don't know about that," he said, remembering the state he'd been in when he learned the news that his family was dead.

"At least you dealt with your grief in a productive way," she said. "Better than how I dealt with mine for the first few years."

"What did you do?" he asked.

"Nothing. Absolutely nothing, except bury myself in a job I hated. It took me a long time to allow myself to live. For the longest time, I couldn't fathom being on this earth without Danny. But eventually, I began to cope. Starting Celebrations, Inc. was the first step toward doing that. You know, other than my girlfriends you're the first person I've talked to about this."

"Not even your family?"

AJ shook her head and swallowed hard. "No, Danny was not my grandmother's choice. So, nobody really talked about my loss. I mean, look at what happened when my mother married my dad. It took him dying before my grandmother would even be civil to my mom. The fact that Danny died before we got married—well, that meant we just didn't talk about it."

Shane wondered at life with a dysfunctional family. He and his family had been so close the opposite dynamic was almost unfathomable. But before he could ask another question, the front-of-the-house team must have finished the dining room setup in short order because they began filtering into the kitchen asking AJ for their next assignments.

After she set them to doing new jobs, she turned to Shane. "Are you ready for this?" She had her work face on again. "It's going to be a busy night."

He nodded. "Just point me in the right direction and tell me what to do. I told you, I've never worked with food before—"

"Not even flipping burgers or in the mess hall?" AJ interrupted.

"Nope. You've got a total food-service virgin on your hands. Be gentle with me?"

He winked, and took a great deal of pleasure watching the color spike in her cheeks. But then she smiled, as if in spite of her embarrassment.

"Noted, but be warned, people say I'm a hellish taskmaster in the kitchen. I hope that doesn't scare you off."

She arched a perfect, dark blond brow and he noticed for the first time that her brows were a couple of shades darker than her light blond hair. The contrast with her blue eyes was striking.

"Me? Scared?" This beautiful woman had him thinking and feeling things he thought he he'd never feel again. He should be petrified. He should walk straight out that door and not look back until he was as far away from her as he could get. He should focus on going back to Italy and his pending discharge. But in the days since he'd met AJ Sherwood-Antonelli the unfinished business he had to take care of in Italy had been the furthest thing from his mind. It seemed to get pushed back even further as he heard himself saying, "I'm a fast and very eager learner. So, I'll think we'll work together just fine. Trust me."

"I'll bet you are," she said. "First, put this on."

She stood in front of him, reached up and looped a white chef's apron around his neck. It took all the willpower he could summon to not put his arms around her waist and draw her close.

Restraint. They were working, and he knew the last thing she needed was for the rest of the waitstaff to catch them cooking up something other than the food on tonight's menu.

Instead, Shane focused on helping AJ finish prepping the green beans, and then concentrated on absorbing the crash course in serving delivered by Benjamin, AJ's head server.

The night went like clockwork. And by the time everything was winding down, he was exhausted. He was glad he'd helped her out, but he was looking forward to returning to the jobsite to familiar territory, rather than being a stranger in the strange land of the kitchen.

It was backbreaking work and the fact that AJ did this for a living—and seemed to thrive on it—deepened his respect for her.

After he'd served the last plate of cake, he headed back to the kitchen over to the sink where AJ was washing a stack of dirty aluminum trays. The others were working in various parts of the kitchen. Two were still in the dining room offering seconds on coffee.

Shane grabbed a dish towel and began drying the items AJ had cleaned.

"So, what's my performance review, boss? Did I measure up tonight?"

She arched a brow at him and there was something seductive in the way she smiled up at him. How could a woman look so damn sexy as she washed dishes?

"Well, let's see…you were quick. You took direction well. Didn't spill anything on anyone. Didn't eat food off the plates. Yeah, I'd hire you again."

"You've seen servers eat food off the plates?"

She rolled her eyes. "You wouldn't believe the things I've witnessed."

"Thanks for cueing me in. The next time I eat out, I'll be on the lookout for grazing waitstaff. I don't mind sharing my food, but I prefer to offer it, or at least have the person ask for a bite."

They laughed, then settled into a companionable silence.

"How about that game of hoops we've been talking about? I seem to remember a challenge that was levied the night before last. How about we play after the town meeting?"

Chapter Eight

They were spending a lot of time together.

AJ contemplated Shane's offer to play basketball as she picked up another dirty pan and lathered it up with dish soap. But spending time together was how people got to know each other.

Even though he wouldn't be in Celebration for the long-term, would it be so bad to enjoy him while he was here? Because one thing was for sure: they did seem to enjoy each other. For God's sake, the guy spent his evening working with her rather than relaxing. Never had a guy gone to such great lengths to spend time with her. It was sweet.

She took a deep breath and gave herself permission to enjoy him. No expectations. Just live a little. Have some fun while he was here.

"That sounds fun," she said. "I'd love to. In fact, how about if I pack us a picnic and we can eat in the park after we finish playing?"

But before he could answer, Pepper came swinging through the kitchen doors. "AJ, there you are. Oh, my God, you're needed in the dining room. Immediately."

"What's wrong?" AJ demanded.

"Nothing is wrong." A huge smile spread across Pepper's face as she noticed Shane. "Well, hello again. We met in the park at the Taste of Celebration Food Festival." She extended her hand, her urgency suddenly transforming into Southern charm.

Shane squeezed her fingers. "Yes, I remember. Pepper, right?"

Pepper shot AJ a coy look. "Good looks and a great memory. I vote we make him a new partner in the business. He did wonders in the dining room tonight. Darlin', you definitely have skills."

Seriously? Had Pepper really said that? AJ shot Shane an embarrassed glance and felt herself blushing on her friend's behalf. "Okay, you said my presence was requested? Right now. Come on, let's go."

Pepper turned on her heel and led the way out of the kitchen. AJ shook her head and shot Shane a dubious look. At least he was smiling.

Given the look on Pepper's face, AJ obviously wasn't being called in for a public berating. Still… she wiped her moist palms on her pants, smoothed her hair and squared her shoulders.

She'd managed to finagle her way out of attending her debutante ball when she was in high school. Tonight, however, she was going to be formally introduced to society…ready or not. No, this time she was ready. It was on her terms and she couldn't be more jazzed.

Or at least she thought so, until she stepped into the dining room and the members of the Women's Club and their guests got to their feet and erupted into a round of enthusiastic applause.

AJ felt her cheeks burn. But not from embarrassment, from pride and passion that couldn't be contained in her heart.

Somehow she knew as she watched the members of her community who had spent a fabulous evening together enjoying the food she'd prepared with love, that everything would be okay. *This* was where she was supposed to be, *this* was what she was supposed to be doing.

She only basked for a moment before her gaze scanned the room searching for the one person whose approval mattered most: Grandmother.

It was easy to find her. She was the only person in the room who was not standing. She wasn't even clapping. No, Agnes Sherwood sat with her hands folded properly in her lap. To anyone else, her expression might have appeared neutral, but AJ could see through her grandmother's society mask to a face that hinted she might smell something slightly foul, but, of course, she was much too *polite* to make a fuss.

AJ's heart sank low in her chest. She reminded herself that tonight, she'd cooked for Pepper and Marjory…when she cooked for her "family" and those closest to her the real essence of her talent came out and infused itself in the food. If her grandmother was embarrassed by the fact that her AJ was doing "…the work of the hired help…" well, she just needed to get over it. Or maybe AJ needed to. Cooking was her calling…. She couldn't please everyone, and that was okay.

After the applause died down, and AJ had accepted the accolades, Florence Lapham, a past Women's Club president and a notable Dallas-area socialite, stopped AJ as she turned to head back to the kitchen.

"Wonderful job, my dear," she said. "Could I get your card, please? My granddaughter is getting married. Unfortunately we have yet to find a satisfactory caterer. Until now. If you could provide something along the lines of what you did for the club tonight—including that delicious cake, my granddaughter will go nuts over—I think we might have hit the jackpot."

A spiral of joy shot through AJ, lighting some of the darkness her grandmother had cast. AJ had come to impress. She'd done her job and done it well. Proof was in the potential business smiling in front of her.

As she thanked the woman and handed her a business card, it dawned on her that even though

Grandmother might not approve, she certainly hadn't incited a boycott, which would've been the quickest way to shut down Celebrations, Inc. Maybe Grandmother's steely exterior wasn't as cold as she'd like for it to appear.

"By the way, the wedding is in three weeks," Florence Lapham informed AJ. It was clear she wasn't asking if AJ was available so much as issuing a sweet Southern advisory. "So reserve the date. We'll need to get together for a tasting as soon as possible. I'll call you tomorrow."

Three weeks! All AJ could do was blink, a knot forming in the pit of her stomach as she watched Mrs. Lapham breeze back into the Women's Club dining hall. How could the bride not have booked a caterer if her wedding was *three weeks* away? It was insane to accept a job on such short notice. But if she could pull it off…

Rephrase: no ifs. She *would* pull it off. And this would cement her business's future. And it would probably be a great first step toward getting Caroline to leave the world of high finance and become her full-time pastry chef/partner.

In the hallway between the dining room and the kitchen, AJ took out her cell phone and dialed Caroline's number.

When she picked up, AJ said, "How fast can you learn to bake and decorate a wedding cake?"

There was silence on the other end of the line. If Caroline hadn't been listening to music, AJ would've thought the call had been dropped, but she heard Jack Johnson singing on about "Banana Pancakes" in background forcing AJ to verbally nudge her friend.

"Caroline, are you there?"

"Yes, I'm here, I went back to the office after I dropped off the cakes and I'm on my way home now. But AJ, I've never baked a wedding cake. I don't know how."

"Well, then we'll learn. Together. Frances Lapham wants to hire Celebrations, Inc. for her granddaughter's wedding if we can provide a red-velvet wedding cake—exactly like what you provided for the dinner tonight—as part of the package. Come on, you have to do it. Please?"

"Oh, AJ..." Caroline sounded weary. "Wedding cakes are a completely different animal than the small cakes I've been making for you. Wedding cakes are big. Big cakes are prone to collapsing. Collapsing wedding cakes destroy catering businesses. I can only think of a few other disasters that could kill a business faster."

"We'll, then we'll just have to practice."

She knew Caroline was exhausted. She'd worked on tonight's cakes all night, delivered them and then went back to work. Now was probably not a good time to expect her to be enthusiastic about more baking. Especially when it involved a learning curve. So, it probably wasn't a good time to mention the tight deadline.

"This is insane," Caroline said, "but you're not going to take no for an answer, are you?"

"You know me too well. When can we get together and start practicing?"

More music-filled silence.

"I don't know. Let me look at my calendar. I can't even think now, I'm so tired."

Fair enough.

"Did you talk to Sydney today?" Caroline asked.

"No. Why? Is everything okay?"

"I don't know. She had more concerns about Texas Star. Called me all in a panic about the way they're asking her to handle the quarterly earnings statement. She said something definitely doesn't smell right."

"Well, Mr. Texas Star himself is here tonight. He's giving away some big scholarships. I mean if they're giving away money, surely things can't be *that* bad."

Caroline made a noise that indicated she wasn't convinced. "It's a tax write-off. But that doesn't mean anything. To a company like Texas Star, giving away a scholarship is like taking a glass of water out of the ocean. I don't know. She's going to come by one night this week and have me look at the quarterly report. So, we'll see. On another note, how did your soldier and his beautiful biceps work out tonight?"

The mention of Shane and his beautiful biceps sent a spiral of awareness surging through AJ. "He did fine." She glanced around to make sure no one could hear her before she said anything else. The muted strains of the evening's speakers filtered in and the people who were in her line of vision seemed to be caught up in the presentation.

"Fine?" Caroline teased. "He was *fine* just standing in the kitchen. But you didn't hire him to be the evening's hot man candy. Or did you?"

AJ leaned against the wall. "You underestimate him. He is way too capable to simply serve as man candy. As Pepper so aptly pointed out, the guy's got skills. You should see those biceps when he busses a tray full of dishes. *Considerable* skills, I'm telling you."

Someone cleared his throat behind her, she turned as Shane brushed past, carrying an empty tray en route to the dining room. He placed it on a tray stand, turned and smiled at her. He was still within earshot.

AJ's mouth went dry. It was one thing for Caroline to say that to him, but it was quite another for him to overhear her repeating it. She changed the subject fast.

"Right. In the meantime, why don't you send me a list of all the things you'll need—pans, decorating items, *everything*—and I'll buy it all. We can set up a time to get together. I'll talk to you later. Bye."

A rushing heat flared through her, a sensation she didn't bother to fight or analyze whether it was embarrassment or simply a general reaction to him. She decided to go with the latter and smiled back at him. He joined her back in the hallway.

"I didn't mean to interrupt your call," he said. "I

was on my way out to the dining room to see if anything else needed to be cleared."

He grinned at her and there was something in his eyes that pulled her right in. Like a tractor beam. But it would be really stupid to get sucked in any more than she already was. Stupid and dangerous, she reminded herself, damming the rising oh-God-how-much-did-he-hear tide of panic.

"Oh, no, you didn't interrupt." She leaped into a recap of what had transpired with Florence Lapham. She told him the wedding was in three weeks and how she and Caroline were on a mission to learn the art of baking wedding cakes.

She was talking way too fast. About nonsense.

"Sounds like a great opportunity. But I'm not surprised. It was one of the best meals I've had in a long time."

The staff had eaten in the kitchen after dessert was served to the clients. It was a perk that AJ included in the compensation. Since she always prepared extra, there was no sense in letting it go to waste.

"Thank you."

Yeah, stupid and dangerous to invest any more of herself…

"Well…" He hitched a thumb toward the dining room. "I'd better get back to work."

"Oh, right." She stepped back to let him pass.

"Don't want to disappoint the boss." He flexed

his biceps and winked at her. "I heard she hired me because I have 'considerable skills.'"

The next day, AJ, Caroline, Sydney and Pepper met for lunch at the Celebrations, Inc. kitchen to strategize for the Lapham wedding. There was no time to waste, and lunch was the only time they could all coordinate their schedules.

"He heard you?" Caroline dropped down onto one of the stainless-steel stools in the kitchen and covered her face with both of her hands. "Oh, my God. That's so embarrassing. I am mortified for you."

AJ shrugged as she set out a bowl of the salad and a platter of sandwiches. Lunch consisted mostly of leftovers from last night's dinner. She'd cut up the remaining Cornish hens and tossed the meat with some curried mayonnaise, added celery, green onion, Golden Delicious apples, raisins, grapes and pecans. She served it on fresh, buttery croissants. The salad was the leftover endive, blue cheese, pears.

"Thanks for the empathy," AJ lamented. "Yeah, it was pretty excruciating."

Pepper set a large vase full of mixed fresh flowers on the counter. They were from a wholesale contact of hers. One of the tasks on their list—in addition to menu variations—was to look at different varieties of flowers and see what they could offer as decorations for the cake.

"What's going on?" Pepper asked.

Sydney set down her purse and briefcase and listened as AJ recounted the story of the embarrassing phone call. When she'd finished, they were all silent for a moment.

Finally, Pepper broke the silence. "This happened last night? Why didn't I know about it until now?"

AJ cringed all over again the sting of embarrassment as fresh as if it had just happened. "Actually, you started it with your 'considerable skills' comment, which I had the bad judgment of repeating. And he overheard me."

"Well, that was…unfortunate."

Sydney shot Pepper a look. "The burning question is what happened next? What did he do?"

"How did he act?" Caroline added.

AJ sighed. "He ribbed me a little, but other than that, he acted like a perfect gentleman. Like nothing was wrong. He's coming to the town meeting tomorrow night. We're playing basketball afterward. And having a picnic. Unless he decides I'm a lunatic and runs for his life."

Sydney shook her head. "I wouldn't write him off just yet."

AJ put four plates on the counter next to the food. "I know. But it just seems so…impossible."

"Why is it impossible?" Caroline demanded.

The room went quiet and her friends waited for an answer. "Because… It's… He's leaving soon. And I'm afraid."

"Honey, you can't let fear hold you back," Pepper said. "You know that. If you didn't, you would've never left Bistro Saint-Germain and started Celebrations. You didn't even have clients or much catering experience, but you fearlessly charged ahead and made it work. Look at you now."

AJ shook her head. "Danny's insurance money and your investment advice are what's getting me through. I was able to quit my day job and open my doors because I have the best friends in the world who believe in me and support me and prop me up when I need to be propped up and—"

"Give you a little nudge when you need to be pushed out of your comfort zone?" Sydney added. "And make sure you don't miss the boat when there's a great guy who seems to be crazy about you."

AJ caught the conspiratorial look her three friends exchanged. "What?"

"Speaking of great guys and pushing you out of your comfort zone," Caroline said. "We have a little present for you."

Pepper pulled a small wrapped package out of her purse. "Here you go. From the three of us, to you."

"What is this for? My birthday is months away."

"Just open it," Sydney said.

As AJ carefully pulled the tape from the colorful, floral-print paper, she sensed something was up. She carefully lifted the wrapping paper and gasped—

"Condoms?" She tossed the unopened box onto the counter as if it would burn her. Or worse. "Oh, my God. What in the hell am I supposed to do with a box of rubbers?"

"Have sex," Pepper said, as matter-of-factly as if it were written in the debutantes' handbook. "That's what you're supposed to do with a box of rubbers. Did your mother not have that talk with you?"

"Need I remind you, this man has *skills,*" Caroline teased. "You told me so yourself, and I had the good fortune to see what's on the surface with my very own eyes."

AJ tried not to squirm.

"Look, honey," Sydney said. "If you're not ready, you don't have to rush into anything. But we thought you should have a little reminder of…all the possibilities. This way you'll be prepared when you are ready."

AJ shook her head and the look on her friend's faces…or maybe it was the thought of actually owning her very own box of condoms—she'd never bought them herself—made her laugh out loud.

Actually, it started as more of a shocked hiccup, but it blossomed into a laugh that was so infectious her friends laughed, too.

"Okay, enough," AJ insisted. "Let's get back to work. We can't hang out here all day and talk about sex. We have a lot to accomplish." She glanced at the abandoned box of condoms, then picked up the box tentatively as if it might burn her. They didn't. She took a small bite of her sandwich, and studied the package as she chewed. The thought of getting intimate with Shane made her shudder. The thought also made her realize he was the first man since Danny she'd ever been interested in dating, much less get *involved* with. Suddenly, the box did feel a little bit hot in her hand. She set it down and picked up her legal pad, redirecting her focus to the business she and her friends needed to discuss.

"I read some articles on baking wedding cakes. From what I can tell we will need cake pans in graduated sizes, dowels, maybe some pillars if she wants a more traditional look, and cake circles."

Caroline nodded. "Right. I have a cake turntable I can donate to the cause and just about every decorating tool known to the confectionery world."

Pepper smiled. "Can you make those cute little roses?"

"You bet I can," said Caroline. "Mr. Biceps isn't the only one with skills."

AJ winced. "Apples and oranges, Caroline." AJ stole another glance at the abandoned box of prophylactics. "Apples and oranges."

They all laughed again.

"Where are you holding the tasting?" Sydney asked.

"The office, of course," AJ said. "Where else would I do it?"

Sydney and Pepper exchanged a look.

"What?" AJ demanded.

"We were afraid you'd want to have it there," said Pepper.

"Why wouldn't I hold it there?" AJ asked. "For a tasting it's a lot easier for them to come to me."

Pepper grimaced. "Where are you planning to put them? In the kitchen or your office?"

The irony in Pepper's voice didn't escape AJ. Her office was the size of a walk-in pantry, and there was no room in the kitchen. "I thought I'd set up a table in the reception area and bring in servers— Why are you shaking your head?"

Pepper sighed and smiled indulgently. "Oh, honey, you're so good at so many things, but there are some areas where you simply don't have a clue."

AJ clucked, but knew better than to take offense. One of the things she loved about her friends was how they were always *real* with her. "Would you care to enlighten me?"

The girls were exchanging looks again. This time, Caroline had joined in on the private joke...or whatever it was they were sharing. Pepper drew in a deep breath and cleared her throat, obviously electing herself spokesperson for the trio.

"Francis Lapham is one of the area's biggest socialites. She is a snob. You cannot set up a card table in that unfinished disaster area that you call a reception area. AJ, there is still exposed drywall."

"What—? Oh!" Suddenly, AJ understood exactly what Pepper was worried about. AJ had been so busy in the kitchen, developing the product, focusing on the food, that she didn't even see the naked drywall she'd had installed to separate the front of the house from the kitchen. Basically, the reception area was still a construction site. Even the most beautifully set table wouldn't camouflage it. How could she not have realized? More important—

"What else am I supposed to do?" The tasting was in three days, hardly enough time to whip the front of the house into shape. Not when she still had some food issues to iron out. She would be a good candidate for a TV show like *Extreme Office Makeovers,* or whatever it was called. But that wasn't going to happen. She'd just have to figure out another plan, even though she was only one person and she was still struggling to perfect the menu for what could be Celebrations' biggest break yet.

Her friends must have read the panic on her face, because Pepper said, "Don't you worry. Just leave everything to us."

AJ hesitated, curious and terrified. "Okay… I guess I don't really have a choice, do I?"

The idea both thrilled and terrified her.

Chapter Nine

Shane liked a lot of things about AJ Sherwood-Antonelli. Besides having won the goddess trifecta—she was smart, funny and beautiful—add to the mix that she was one hell of a great cook. The combination was enough to bring a man to his knees.

He also liked the way her nose wrinkled when she laughed. He loved how she didn't flinch or look away when he sometimes caught her looking at him. She might smile, quirk a brow, but her direct gaze never wavered. There was strength in those blue eyes that moved him. Like an earthquake ripping open solid rock.

Tuesday, as he sat at his desk with his morning coffee, pondering the many qualities of AJ, he also found himself scrolling through the contacts in his cell and pausing when he found her number.

There had been plenty of women who had come and gone in his life—women who lived in the various cities, states and countries he happened through on his assignments during his time in the army. He'd known more than his fair share of wonderful, beautiful women. But those affairs usually lasted the stint of his tour. When it was time to move, it was time to move on. He served everyone well by keeping those affairs passionate but unemotional.

He knew the problems that came with letting his heart get involved. And he saved everyone a lot of grief and heartache by being very up front about his intentions, or lack thereof.

So why was it he found himself thinking nonstop about AJ? What was it about her that made him feel things he thought he was incapable of feeling, that had him rethinking his don't-get-involved code?

Probably the same thing that drove him to dial her number and invite her to visit the job site. Well, they'd talked about it the night they went to dinner at Taco's. So, why not now?

"If you're free after work, why don't you stop by? I'll give you a tour of the job site." It sounded like a thinly veiled excuse to see her, which it was, but that didn't matter when she walked through the construction trailer door just before five-thirty, looking way too sexy all dressed up in a silky royal blue dress and high heels. She greeted him with a hug.

When she pulled away, he gave her another once-over. Not exactly construction-zone attire. Still, he heard himself uttering, "You look great," amazed at how the woman could transform from no-nonsense businesswoman and boss in her white chef's coat, to someone who looked as if she'd be perfectly at home in that other life her grandmother wanted her to live.

"Did you get all dressed up for me?" he asked only half joking.

She slanted him a flirtatious glance. "Actually, I can't stay long because there's something I have to do tonight. But speaking of being dressed up...look at you in your uniform."

His mind was stuck on the something or someone that was claiming her tonight. A pang of disappointment stabbed him. He'd hoped that after he walked her around the job site, they might grab a bite to eat. He felt a little off-kilter for being so presumptuous thinking she'd automatically be free. A strange feeling of possessiveness simmered in him, foreign and sort of...Neanderthal-like. He knew he had no right, no claim on her, but—

"So this is your office?" she said.

A fluorescent light buzzed and flickered as she looked around the small construction trailer, turning in a full circle as she took in everything. He looked, too, trying to see it through her eyes: the walls that were covered in dated, blond paneling; the drafting table covered with blueprints; the cheap credenza with a coffeemaker, packets of sugar and sugar substitutes stuffed in a foam cup, and bottles of powdered creamer. Shane's desk was across from the door.

She nodded. "It's nice finally seeing where you disappear to every day."

All he could think about was where she might be disappearing tonight.

The two-hour tasting with Florence Lapham and her granddaughter, Jade, couldn't have gone better, and AJ collapsed into her office chair with proof in hand: a signed contract to cater Jade's wedding. The Lapham ladies seemed truly pleased with the menu selections they'd tasted and had narrowed it down to a sumptuous feast that would start with an assortment of canapés—seared Ahi Tuna, Bloody Mary shooters garnished with jumbo cocktail shrimp, and Belgian endive stuffed with Boursin cheese and hearts of palm—carried among the guests as they waited for the bride and groom to arrive at the reception. Then the party would sit down to a watercress salad and a choice of beef Wellington or lobster tail, accompanied by roasted seasonal root vegetables, and grilled herbed fingerling potatoes. Caroline's red-velvet cake had sealed the deal.

It had all fallen into place perfectly. Not only had she wowed them with the food, but Pepper and Sydney had worked magic on the front of the house at the Celebrations, Inc. offices. Using bolts of silk and gossamer organza they'd transformed the ugly, bare drywall into a bride's paradise. They'd rigged a crystal chandelier Pepper had procured from who knows where; they'd carried in dozens of flowers, topiaries, candles and twinkling lights. Their handiwork had visions of an event-planning division of Celebrations, Inc. dancing through AJ's mind. What would she do without them? She didn't plan on finding out.

Arms full of containers of leftover cake and food from the tasting, she stepped out of the office into the dark, crisp Texas night toward her car. She'd only taken a few steps when she glanced back over her shoulder to admire the way the reception area looked through the storefront windows.

It was so beautiful, it took her breath away. She turned around to admire the way the silk and gossamer shimmered in the glow of the twinkle lights. Why hadn't she thought of doing something this before? In fact, how on earth could she have ever thought of serving Mrs. Lapham and Jane in the reception area in its pre-makeover condition?

After clearing away the dishes from the tasting, she'd spruced up the stage Pepper and Sydney had set and left the twinkle lights on so people could admire the beautiful picture it made.

No doubt about it, she was as giddy as if she were the bride herself. She shifted the boxes of leftovers so that she had a better hold on them. She really should call Syd and Pepper to thank them…again. And she needed to call Caroline to tell her how much they loved the cake, but it had been ten-thirty when she'd locked up the office. Pepper and Sydney were at a Texas Star function tonight. Caroline was probably still working. She vowed to call them first thing tomorrow morning. Plus, if she were completely honest, the person she really wanted to talk to right now was Shane. She couldn't wait to tell him about her success.

With one last wistful glance at her shop window, she turned and walked toward her car. Just then a red Honda sped past, way too fast. The driver must have been doing at least fifty miles per hour in the twenty-five-mile-an-hour zone.

"Whoa! Slow down, buddy. Where are you off to in such a hurry?" Her shop was in the business district. All of the stores and offices were closed at this hour and there wasn't much traffic, but it irritated her when people broke the rules. That's how accidents happened. She didn't recognize the car, but then again, she knew most every single person who called Celebration home, but not all. Shaking her head, she watched the Honda's taillights disappear down the street.

As she continued her trek to the car, irritation about the reckless driver got lost in the glow over tonight's success, and, of course, the memory of Shane in his uniform. Thoughts of him had lived in the back of her mind all evening. If he had looked delicious in a civilian polo shirt, his camouflage fatigues made him look tempting enough to eat. She'd always felt at ease around him, but this evening, she'd been a little tongue-tied seeing him looking so official.

That's why she'd been cryptic about her plans for the evening. If she'd failed to land the job... She blinked away the thought. Still, in retrospect, she realized winning the Lapham wedding was a huge stretch for a relatively inexperienced caterer. It was a reality she hadn't let herself fully acknowledge for fear that one iota of negativity might cost her. This job done right would put her business on the Dallas/Celebration social map. She would do everything in her power to ensure that Jade Lapham had the wedding dinner of her dreams.

She couldn't wait to share the good news with Shane.

As she used the remote fob to unlock her car door, she noticed the same red Honda that had sped by a moment ago pass by again. This time it was going slower. About ten yards past her office, the car stopped, idling in the middle of the street. AJ craned her neck to see the license plate number, but it was a little too far away for her to read clearly.

Was that an N9DK or M40R? Shesh, I need to get my eyes checked. She took a few steps toward the car to see if she could read the tag better.

She couldn't. What she could see, however, was that the Honda had fancy wheels—"tricked out" was the expression she'd heard her twelve-year-old nephew use to describe cars that had been...err... fixed up. In the next instant, the car sped away. The squeal of burning rubber sliced through the still night air.

As the silence settled around her again, it brought with it an uneasiness that made the hair on her arms stand on end. *Kids,* she thought, trying to reassure herself. It's just a kid trying to be cool.

The same kids who set fire to the brush in the square?

Not wanting to be standing there if the vehicle made a third pass down the street, she got into her car, locked her door, and started the engine. Should she call the sheriff? If so, what would she say? That a red Honda had been driving too fast, and then it stopped? No laws broken. No property damaged. Her own peace of mind a little worse for the wear, perhaps. But really nothing worth bothering the sheriff over. Instead, she would mention the incident at the town hall meeting tomorrow night and make others aware.

Yes, that's what she'd do. She buckled her seat belt. For now, she had to put it out of her mind. To help with that, she dialed Shane's number via the hands-free device built into her car.

When he answered, she said, "I understand you come highly recommended in the catering world because you're considerably skilled."

He chuckled. "Is that the word on the street?" His voice was sexy and low. The sound made her melt a little inside, and she instantly knew why thoughts of him had possessed her tonight—visions of a man in uniform…or *out* of uniform—

Oh, no, I did not just think that.

Oh, yes I did.

She smiled to herself as she started for home, enjoying the contrast of the heat of her flushed cheeks against the cool night air. It made her shiver. Shane was so much fun to flirt with. The thrill of the blush and the rush of flirting in the darkened privacy of her car…

"Yeah, that's what they're saying. Are you available for a wedding on October 8?"

"Why, are you proposing?" he asked.

"Maybe I am." She smiled, trying to think of a wittier comeback, until she realized the stoplight she'd just driven through was a very hot yellow. She needed to quit daydreaming about Shane and keep her mind on the road. Glancing in her rearview mirror, she saw that the car behind her hadn't bothered to stop, either. He was right behind her, tailgating. No doubt, by that time, the light had been the same shade as his car—red.

The red Honda.

AJ's heart hammered. Even though the car's side windows were tinted, which meant she'd been unable to see in as the car was parked by her office, now the car was following so closely behind her that she could make out at least two guys in the front seat. They looked young. Though she couldn't be completely certain, she had a sinking feeling they were among the boys who didn't get caught the night of the fire in the park.

That's when she began to panic.

"This is going to sound really crazy." Her voice shook a little. "But I think I'm being followed."

She relayed the story of the car's double pass down Robinson Street, how it had stopped and then sped off. She told him that from a distance, it looked like it could be some of the guys from the other night in the park.

"I don't like the sound of this," Shane said. "Are you near the sheriff's station?"

"Not really. Actually, I'm only a couple of blocks from home."

She tightened her grip on the wheel.

"Whatever you do, don't go home. Instead, make a series of left turns to make sure it's not just a coincidence."

She did as Shane advised. "He's still behind me."

"Drive to the sheriff's office right now. Just go. I'll meet you there."

The following morning, Shane came over and picked up AJ and took her to get her car. They'd left it parked at the sheriff's station. Shane hoped it would serve as a reminder to the thug in the red Honda that he'd better not mess with her.

He'd wanted her to come home with him, but she'd shyly refused—even though her vibe suggested she might be tempted. He hadn't expected her to say yes.

Still, he'd offered and he'd hoped. But it was probably for the best that they didn't get physically involved. He was leaving sooner than he wanted to admit, and AJ wasn't a short-term fling.

So instead of her spending the night at his place, he'd driven her home in his truck. They'd refused the offer for the sheriff to follow them home and secure the perimeter of AJ's house. Shane hadn't thought it a bad idea, but AJ had argued that a cop car outside her home would draw too much attention.

"That's what this expensive burglar alarm I invested in is for. Plus, I think the guy—or guys, whatever the case may be—are just punks. If they're trying to scare me because I talked to the sheriff after one of them set fire in the park, I refuse to let them win. Me staying with you, or you staying with me and the sheriff getting involved would mean they'd won."

Really, he couldn't argue with that.

After he'd taken her to get her car, they'd agreed to meet at the town hall meeting for the neighborhood watch kickoff.

Even though it wasn't his neighborhood, Shane had some concerns at the construction suite, and after what had happened with the punks, as AJ had called them, trying to scare her last night, Shane intended to go and at least put in his two cents.

Shane had zero tolerance for punks, vandals and bullies, because that lot had a tendency to graduate into careers as hardened criminals—or worse yet, terrorists who killed innocent people for sport.

By the time he got to the community center where the meeting was being held, it was standing room only.

He'd had to work a little later than he'd expected, so he didn't have time to go home and change clothes. Instead, he wore his uniform. When he walked in, heads turned and people shot him curious glances. He was used to that when he was in a largely civilian community. Nothing screamed *stranger* louder than a man in uniform. Thank goodness AJ waved at him from the front. She'd saved him a seat. He wove though the crowd and made his way up front.

"There you are." She stood and gave him a hug. "I was hoping you'd make it."

"Are you kidding? After last night, I wouldn't miss it. Everything okay today?"

She stiffened and her smile faded. She looked vulnerable for a split second. "The sheriff told me they found out the red Honda we saw last night was stolen."

Apparently, AJ had given them enough info—even with her nearsighted misreading of the tags—that they were able to call up the records.

AJ breathed in and shut her eyes. Then, when she opened them she raised her chin a little and nodded resolutely. "Everything will be fine."

"Yes, it will," Shane said. "I'll make sure of it." And he meant that.

Everyone took their seats and the meeting started. AJ and Shane, along with a handful of people, shared their stories and concerns. The representative from the sheriff's office instructed them on how to set up the watch program. The group elected neighborhood captains—the ones who would be in charge of gathering names, addresses and phone numbers of the residents in their designated areas and distributing lists so that the citizens could stay in touch. Signs would go up around town next week advising that crime would not be tolerated in Celebration, Texas.

In the meantime, residents were advised to be aware of their surroundings. Know their neighbors. Look out for each other and report anything suspicious.

The meeting was short and sweet. Now, Shane was looking forward to helping take AJ's mind off last night's scare by finally having the opportunity to play their long-awaited game of hoops. And, of course, she'd packed a picnic for them to enjoy in the park afterward.

"Are you ready to go?" Shane asked.

"Yes, let's get out of here," AJ said.

He put his hand on the small of her back and helped maneuver her through the lingering crowd.

They'd almost made it to the door, when Shane felt a hand on his shoulder.

He turned to see Agnes Sherwood, peering down her nose at him.

"Oh, hi, Grandma," AJ said. "I didn't realize you were here tonight."

"Hello, dear." Agnes spoke to AJ, but her unwavering gaze scrutinized Shane. She was sizing him up. "Yes, I was sitting in the back. So, you're the one who helped Agnes Jane last night."

"Yes, ma'am. It was the least I could do."

She nodded, with no expression on her drawn face. "I appreciate you looking after her. You are the same person I met at the food festival, correct? The unfortunate one whom my granddaughter doused with barbecue sauce?"

"Yes, that guy is me, and I must say, I love AJ's barbecue sauce."

Agnes made a noise somewhere between a *humph* and a grunt, and Shane saw AJ tense up. It probably wasn't noticeable to anyone else, but it didn't escape Shane.

"Grandma, it was nice to see you," AJ said, crisply, "but we need to be going. We have plans."

"You have a date?" Agnes asked. "Where?"

"We are playing basketball, and then we're feasting on a picnic of leftovers from a tasting I did last night."

Shane had never actually seen a person's nose curl in disgust…until now.

"Really, Agnes Jane? Basketball is such a vulgar sport. It's so unladylike and common. Please don't embarrass me by acting like a street urchin."

With another *humph-grunt,* Agnes turned and

walked away. If Shane thought he'd scored some points at the start of this encounter, he definitely felt as though AJ's grandmother had found him lacking in the end, taking her granddaughter on such a "vulgar" date. But he didn't care. With all due respect, Agnes was not invited on the date.

Shane glanced at AJ, who was shooting daggers with her eyes at her grandmother's back.

"Shane, I'm so sorry." Glancing back at him, she looked mortified. "I really believe my grandmother meant well. At least, at first. If it's any conciliation, I've never heard my grandmother thank anyone before. Especially not a guy I was interested in."

Wait. What? Back up there. Shane wanted to ask her to repeat that last part. The part about the "guy she was interested in." But he didn't. Instead, he tried to lighten her mood. "Personally, I'll accept your grandmother's expression for what it is. Gratitude. She may not know how to express it, but I sense she's relieved that you're okay."

And, by the way, the guy you're interested in says the feeling's mutual.

AJ shrugged. "I guess so. She just had an awful way of expressing it."

"So, I'll take the good and toss out what doesn't work. Okay? Now, how about we go shoot some hoops, *Agnes Jane?*"

"It's AJ to you, mister," she said as she went in low and smooth and stole the basketball right out of

Shane's hands. "Especially after I just picked your pocket like that."

"Pocket picker," he shouted and laughed as she dunked the ball. "I think I'll alert the neighborhood watch captain."

"Oooh, well, if you insist on trash talking, I have to remind you that *Grandmother* does have you pegged as a transient since you're living in the pay-by-the-week projects."

Shane went for the rebound. "Technically, I am transient and I am living in the pay-by-the-week projects. You say that like it's a bad thing."

"I didn't say it, Grandmother did."

AJ caught the ball and skirted Shane for another dunk.

He laughed. "When I was younger, we used to joke about people who invested all their money in fancy cars and didn't save anything for the future, and still lived with their mama. At least I drive a fancy truck and live in an apartment. That shows that my priorities aren't out of whack."

It was supposed to be a joke. The whole trash-talking round of hoops was supposed to be all in fun. But it made her think about how Shane had lost his family. She racked her brain for something funny to steer the conversation in another direction.

But by that time they were both out of breath.

"This was a great workout," AJ said. "Why don't we take a break and eat? I don't know about you, but suddenly I'm starving."

"Me, too," Shane agreed.

They got the picnic basket and a small cooler out of her car and found a grassy spot under a tree that was dripping with Spanish moss. They spread out the blue-and-red-plaid blanket, and AJ set to work preparing the plates with what remained of the Lapham tasting. As any good caterer with an eye for hospitality would do, she'd made more than enough. Frances and Jade had eaten their fill and there was just about enough left for two more meals. More than enough, but nothing would go to waste.

"Sorry to serve you leftovers," she said. "But honestly, the flavors are always better the next day."

She garnished the plate with parsley and vegetables that had been cut and curled and handed a plate to Shane.

"This doesn't look like the leftovers I ate when I was growing up. And now, most of my leftovers come from a takeout container or a doggy bag. This food looks fit for a society wedding."

AJ smiled. Oh, how she loved food and the effect it had on people. That was because every dish she created was infused with her passion for cooking. She watched Shane as he was enjoying a bite of cold lobster salad that she'd made from the leftover lobster tails, and the sheer bliss on his face as he chewed made her want to fall in love.

The thought unleashed a swarm of butterflies, flying in figure-eight formation in her stomach. She'd fed plenty of people since Danny had died, but the possibly of dating, much less giving her heart away again, hadn't seemed in the realm of available options.

The sensible part of her wanted to pull back, play it safe. But the butterflies had already flown off with her heart and even the sensible part of her couldn't do a thing to stop it.

She took a deep breath against the rush.

Oh, no, this was not good.

It was absolutely wonderful.

Dusk was beginning to fall, bringing with it a cool breeze and a melancholy sunset. To bring herself back to earth, she lit some small votive candles and said, "Tell me about your childhood—and those leftovers you ate when you were growing up."

Shane stopped midbite, fork poised in front of his mouth. He set the fork on his plate and seemed to be contemplating the question.

"If you don't mind talking about it. I know losing your family must have been an incredible shock. But I'm sure they played a big part in forming you into the person you are, and I was just wondering if you wanted to talk about them."

She, of course, would have to be willing to talk about Danny. And she was willing. In fact, it seemed as if telling Shane about him might be a way to get Danny's blessing before exorcising his ghost. She didn't want to forget about him, but she needed to set her heart free from the shackles that had been holding her back.

"My mother was incredible—both of my parents were, actually—but my mom was completely selfless. Pretty much lived her life for her kids. We'd just moved back to Italy that summer after I graduated from high school and she was all excited about exposing us to European culture. She wasn't a very good cook, but she'd decided she was going to take some cooking classes once we got settled in. She never got a chance."

There were a million things AJ wanted to say: *I feel your pain—or at least a version or your pain. The part that knows how loss bores a hole in your soul; I'm Italian. Or at least the part of me that my grandmother hates is*. More important than talking about herself, though, she wanted to hear about him.

"Why did you stay in Italy when your family flew back to the States?" She hadn't meant to say that out loud and held her breath after the words slipped out.

"There was a girl…a young woman, I guess I should say. We were young. I was stupid. Thought I was in love. I didn't want to leave her. That's pretty much all there is to say."

The look on his face made a lump form in her throat. She'd asked for it—she'd sensed that this was what he would say. Or some version of that same story. She'd felt it in her bones.

"And you're going back to Italy? You'd mentioned it would be your last assignment."

He nodded.

There was one more thing she needed to know…a

last piece of the puzzle that she had to fill in and if she didn't ask now, she might not get the chance… more likely she might chicken out.

"Have you been in touch with the woman?"

She felt her walls go up, preparing for an answer she didn't want to hear.

Shane shook his head.

AJ exhaled, giving voice to the most critical part of the question.

"Are you going back to find her?"

Before he could answer, the wail of emergency sirens burst the silence. Then AJ's cell phone rang. She glanced at the caller ID. The pit of her stomach dropped to her toes.

"I'm sorry, I'd better take this call. It's the fire department!"

Chapter Ten

"It's definitely arson," said the fire chief. "We found traces of gasoline around back at the hotspot where the fire started."

Shane put a firm arm around AJ as she stood stoic and numb staring at the ruin that used to be Celebrations, Inc.

Her shop was gone. And with it, her whole life—everything she'd worked so hard for—had vanished with the flames. Everything inside was burned beyond recognition—all her equipment, her files, the gossamer and silk that had brought the storefront to life was now reduced to soot and ash along with her hopes and dreams.

Where was she going to find a space in the span

of a week that would allow her to cater the Lapham wedding? She needed large ovens, portable ovens.

Now, she had nothing.

Who in the world would do such a despicable thing like set fire to someone else's property?

She had no enemies. Who in the world would do this to her?

Her mind raced back to the gang of teens in the park. To the one who was arrested for setting the fire. To the red Honda that she had shrugged off despite the warnings.

Was it a vendetta for giving a report to the sheriff that led to the gang member's arrest?

The thought made her so sick to her stomach she started to shake. It was either that or retch. Shane pulled her closer, and she wasn't about to lose her dinner on his shoes.

There really was no safe haven in this world, was there?

Not in the big city. Not in the small town where she'd grown up, the place she'd come back to after losing Danny. But this place wasn't safe, either.

She'd gotten a false sense of security because she was shrouded by her alarm systems and the newly established neighborhood watch program that she was protected. The same way she thought bulletproof vests would protect Danny.

They didn't.

Now she stood there helpless, wondering if she could ever feel safe anywhere in the world. Right now, she just wanted to disappear into the sanctuary of Shane's arms. But that wasn't safe, either. There were still too many unanswered questions. And the one that answered them all was the fact that he was leaving. For Italy. For whatever it was that had a hold on him there.

Still, just for tonight, she had no other place to seek refuge *but* in Shane's arms. So, when he insisted on staying with her that night, this time she didn't refuse.

"It's up to you," he said. "You can come to Houdini's and my luxurious rent-by-the-week digs..." He paused, obviously trying to make her laugh. She gave it her best try, but the sound came out a dry, humorless chuckle. He gave her another squeeze. "Or why don't we come to you? Come on, I'll drive you home."

All the way home, AJ sat on the truck's bench seat sandwiched between Shane, who had one arm around her as he drove, and Houdini, who sat on her right, leaning into her, occasionally looking up and whining as if to assure her that he empathized with her pain and was there. Numbly, she stroked his soft fur. The feel of his warm, fuzzy body so close to her and Shane on the other sine was reassuring. For a moment it felt like this might be the one safe place on earth. Until her thoughts strayed off in rogue directions, traveling to places like how women were raised to believe in fairy tales, that if they're perfect enough and worked hard enough someday they'd be rewarded with their heart's desire, they'd be swept off their feet by a handsome prince and live happily ever after in their ivory tower where they had everything they'd ever wanted or needed. But nobody talked about how dreams went up in smoke and how the ivory tower wasn't impenetrable. People destroyed hard-won dreams and men left…one way or another, they always left.

She knew she wasn't in a good place right now. She really should just keep her mouth shut. But she wanted to lose herself in Shane tonight. She wanted him to hold her until the entire world and all the heartache and disappointment faded into oblivion. And she was going to do just that. The only problem was the very distant shred of reason that didn't seem to be numb and was in touch with reality—barely—and reminded her that he was leaving, too. If he became her sanctuary, that would eventually be taken from her, as well.

"You're really going to leave, aren't you?" she asked.

"What do you mean?"

"You're going to Italy after your work is done here and you're probably never coming back, right?"

He wavered a moment. "I have to go. I don't have a choice."

"Yes, you do," she insisted. "We always have a choice. Saying you don't is a cop-out."

At a stop sign, he slid his arm from her shoulders

and put both hands on the wheel. He stared straight ahead out the windshield.

"In the army, you really don't have a choice. I have to go where they send me. But I'm done in a matter of months. We can see where we are once we get to that point."

She was an idiot for being so combative. She really shouldn't try to pick a fight. But maybe this was the only way to quash the chemistry, to drive distance between them so that she wouldn't wake up in the morning having done something that she'd regret. For an instant, she wished she could be the kind of woman who could distance her heart and soul from the physical act of sex. She wished she could be the type to lose herself in down-and-dirty, mindless sex for the sheer escape of it.

Even if it was a temporary escape.

But because it would be temporary, and the spell of forgetting would fade fast, she knew she… couldn't.

"Why Italy, Shane?"

Then he slanted her a look. His gaze was narrowed, but not in an antagonistic way.

"It's hard to explain. Other than I guess recently I've felt I needed to go back to the beginning—where all the hurt and pain started—before I could put it behind me. For a while, I thought if I just moved on, kept going, someday I could forget. But that was my *family,* AJ. I lost them in one terrible accident that didn't have to happen. A lot like what's happened to you. Sort of. I guess you could compare the two."

Her heart sank at the thought that he would downplay the loss of his family to make her feel better. The comparison was a sobering awakening. Of course, it was about healing. He deserved to be able to do whatever it took to heal. "Bricks, mortar and business plans can be replaced, flesh and blood can't," she said. "I'm so sorry for that. I'm sad and really pissed off at whoever did this, but thinking about your family really helps put things into perspective."

And the woman…? She wanted to ask, but she couldn't. She'd already put her foot in her mouth.

"Her name was Manuela, in case you were wondering. I haven't seen her since the accident—more than twenty years ago. But I do have to admit, I'd been curious about her. Before I met you, I thought that maybe, just maybe if I went back over there and she was somehow free…that maybe that would be key to closure. Eh, that sounds so stupid now, when I say it aloud. Twenty years. She probably has kids and a husband. A family, which I guess is all I've wanted since I lost mine. I just didn't realize it until now."

At the next light, he slid his arm around her again and pulled her close. They rode in silence for a while. Until he said, "Come with me to Italy."

What? Her heart hiccupped. He was asking her to go with him… *Really?* No. She couldn't. She had so much to do—insurance claims, finding a new space or rebuilding that one…

She laid her head on his shoulder. “Shane, you know I can’t.”

“Sure you can. It’s your choice.”

His invitation wasn’t insincere. In her heart, she believed that. But she had to wonder if he was calling her bluff. She’d told him he was copping out earlier when he said he didn’t have a choice. Was he transferring the fate of their relationship onto her shoulders? The point that she was trying to make was the reason it was a bad idea for her to lose her heart to him: he couldn’t stay, she couldn’t leave. He had another year in the army, another assignment. Her business was here. So were her family, her friends.

What if she said yes, that she’d go? Was he really trying to find a way to make this work, or was he simply trying not to be the bad guy?

“You know I can’t leave now. Especially after all that has just happened.”

“AJ, is staying here for *your* career any more of a cop-out than me following where mine leads me?”

No. Yes… *Ahh,* but see he *was* testing her. Her heart sank low in her chest.

They pulled into her driveway and sat there for a moment with the engine running and the lights shining on the garage door.

“So all along, your plan was to make me fall in love with you even though this is an impossible situation?”

“No. I wasn’t planning on anything like that.” His

expression turned serious as his gaze knotted with hers. "But are you?"

"Am I what?"

"In love with me?"

She felt utterly transparent. She knew the answer was written all over her face, but she couldn't bring herself to say the words. Because what was the use? Her feelings for him were her own fault. She'd let him in even though she knew he was leaving. This wasn't going to work out the way she'd hoped and the sooner she accepted it, the better off they'd both be.

"Thank you for everything," she said. "But I'm really tired. I'm going to bed. You and Houdini can sleep in the guest room."

She led him down the hall and turned on the light. "This is it. There are sheets on the bed. The bathroom is off the hall. There are towels in the linen closet in the bathroom. I'll show you how to set the alarm. After you take Houdini out, I'd appreciate it if you turned it on. Especially after tonight."

He was being really quiet, watching her, but not saying a word. Outwardly, he appeared calm, but the tick in his jaw belied his facade.

"I meant what I said about you coming to Italy with me," he finally said. "A lot's happened tonight. I want you to think about it."

"Shane, you know I can't."

He held up a hand as if to fend off her words. "Don't answer me now. Just think about it."

Then they were standing face-to-face with nothing but good-night between them.

He put her arms around her and pulled her to him until their lips barely brushed.

For a moment, AJ went very still, but she wasn't about to pull away. Her patience was rewarded when he deepened the kiss, pulling her even tighter against him.

Every part of her sighed with want, and suddenly, she knew she needed him desperately. Judging by the way he was holding on to her, he needed her, too. She leaned in even closer, pressing against him, closing all space between them so that she could feel the heat of his body through their clothes. Still, her desire and yearning weren't satisfied. She needed more from him.

As if reading her mind, he tightened his grip on her and she felt his strength encircle her, hot as a ring of fire.

He pulled away a little and muttered something that sounded an awful lot like, "Damn." He whispered the words right over her lips before he kissed her again, this time with the same punishing need she was feeling for him.

Fire, white-hot and intense, shot through her, starting at the seam where their lips met and plunging all the way to her toes that were curled in her Dr. Martens.

For a few moments, she forgot the fear and danger of the fire, of losing herself in him. Fervently, she pushed the thought out of her head, then she slipped her hands under his shirt so that she could feel the heat of his body and explore the solid, hard-as-steel sinew of his muscles.

He pulled back a little, his forehead resting on hers. "You know where this is leading, don't you?"

Overcome with emotion and conflict because, yes, she knew and she wanted him with every fiber in her being, she turned her head, allowing herself some space, some room to breathe. But she could still smell him and taste him and her body demanded more.

He made a low, barely perceptible sound deep in his throat. She understood that he was just as consumed as she was by the passion that coursed between. But the reality was their days together were numbered. She couldn't just drop everything and go to Italy.

Think about it, he'd said.

No. Right now, it was the last thing she wanted to think about. She didn't want to think about anything. Especially when he pulled her to him again and his mouth came down on hers.

She wanted the hot, hungry kisses to last forever. Because of that she quit thinking, quit fighting and melted into him, letting their heat fuse and ignite, envelop them in the flames their passion stoked.

The fleeting thought that they should stop passed through his mind. He should be the strong one and leave because she was vulnerable right now, and he didn't want to take advantage of her fragile state of mind. But the feel of her body against his—that heady combination of female softness giving way to firm male resistance—blurred the edges of what he should do and what his body craved.

She wanted him to stay.

He wanted her to feel safe.

Wasn't that enough reason to stay?

The part of him that was cognizant and registered the way her lips responded to his kisses placated his conscience. The way she was kissing him back fed his appetite, until there was no sense in fighting it. It was simply too powerful to ignore. He drank her in as if she were wine, and he was intoxicated by the sheer essence of her.

Finally, when he feared he might drown in the sweetness of her lips, he released her, resting his head against hers, closing his eyes against the urges that threatened to overtake him.

"I can't go to Italy." Her voice was a hushed murmur of bewildered anguish. "I can't leave. You can't stay. What are we going to do, Shane?"

Her words sobered him, pulling him back to the present, forcing him to fight the undertow of yearning that had swept them both out into an emotional sea that was way over their heads.

After steadying himself, he pulled back and studied her face. Her eyes were dark with passion and she looked slightly breathless.

He drew in a deep breath as something new and

fragile flooded through him. He couldn't remember ever feeling such tenderness for a woman. Sure, he'd cared for others, but he'd never experienced the deep, soul-rending tenderness he was feeling for her right now.

What the hell were they going to do?

Released her gently, he swallowed hard and said, "We really should say good-night."

He saw her blink a few times, as if to regain her bearings. She smoothed her hair off her face with hands that shook ever so slightly. At that moment he wanted nothing more than to scoop her up and carry her to his bed where he could finish what they'd started.

But this wasn't the time.

Thank God he'd be able to salvage his senses.

"Good night, AJ. I'll be right across the hall if you need me."

Chapter Eleven

She tried to look casual as he said good-night, but she had to work at the nonchalance. Her smile felt pasted on. "See you in the morning."

She walked toward her room knowing she needed to leave now. If she didn't… Well, she knew exactly where they'd end up.

As she headed down the hall toward her bedroom, she glanced back, over her shoulder. But he wasn't behind her. She kept walking, feeling foolish for hoping he'd be there. He'd offered to stay to give her peace of mind. That certainly didn't mean he'd come with the intention of ending up in her bed. He wasn't the kind of guy who took advantage of a fragile situation and that was one of the many reasons she was falling in love with him.

She paused in the threshold of her bedroom, biting her bottom lip, trying to erase the feel of his kiss. She listened. But all was quiet except for the soft hum of the air conditioner and the occasional rattle of Houdini's tags. He'd obviously made short order of settling in for the night.

Inside her room with the door shut, the quiet felt oppressive. As her ears adjusted to the silence, she could hear the faint symphony of the cicadas outside. It was one of those sounds that could go unnoticed until you heard it, and once you did it seemed to grow louder with every second. She wanted to put her hands over her ears to block out the noise, but even that felt as if it required too much effort.

Uggh…her office was…gone. She felt miserable. Absolutely alone and miserable.

But as she searched for a silver lining, she realized at least she wasn't scared. He might not be in her bed, but he wouldn't let the boogie man get in.

She took a long shower and dressed in a short nightgown. Before she slid between the cool sheets, she turned off the light and twisted opened the blinds so that they slanted up enough for her to see outside. In bed, she turned over onto her side and stared out into the dark of night. A flicker of lightning flashed across the sky illuminating a bank of sullen clouds. A rumble of thunder sounded as angsty as she felt.

She hoped it would rain, that the sky would open up and the heavens would cry. Because that's exactly what she wanted to do. But she'd stored the tears away for so long, she'd forgotten how to let down.

Instead, she felt the anger of what had happened tonight coursing in her veins. These punks weren't mere vandals now, they were criminals and their handiwork would set her back. What the heck was she supposed to do about her business? About the Lapham wedding next week?

Because of these amateur terrorists, she had to have a man sleep in her spare bedroom for protection and she couldn't even open her bedroom window and listen to the approaching storm or the smell the showers moving in, that loamy, earth scent of decay and renewal.

She'd always loved thunderstorms—even as a child. As long as everyone she loved was inside, safe from the elements, a good, hard rain seemed to put another barrier of protection between them and the outside world. Not that she had to worry about protection in those days…before her father and Danny had died. Before the wacko who'd tried to set her office on fire had finished upending what little of her life she'd managed to put back together.

No, tonight, she would not open her windows to welcome the storm. If she did, the rekindled fear might very well consume what was left of her.

She closed her eyes and listened to the rumble of the thunder, and let her mind drift to happier times.

Later that night, a sound roused AJ from her fitful sleep. At first, she thought it was the thunder, but before she closed her eyes, light streaming in from the hall silhouetted a tall figure in the threshold of her bedroom door. The door that had been closed before she went to sleep.

She jerked awake. White-hot fear rushed through her veins, pinning her to the mattress, holding her perfectly still. But it couldn't stop her mind from racing.

What the hell should she do? Turn on the lamp on the bedside table? Make a grab for the pepper spray that was in her purse on the chair across the room?"

Her heart hammered so loudly, she was certain it was echoing throughout the room. But then her eyes adjusted to the silhouette, and her brain registered the red T-shirt. *Shane's* red T-shirt. She sat up.

"Shane?" Her voice shook.

"Yes, it's okay," he said. "It's just me."

"You scared me to death. What are you doing?"

"I'm sorry. I was just checking on you."

AJ blew out a sigh as a rush of adrenaline and relief made her flop down onto the mattress.

Shane hesitated for a minute, then sat down on the edge of her bed.

"I didn't mean to scare you," he said.

She pressed her palms to her eyes for a few seconds, and then she felt steady again. "No, it's okay. I wasn't really asleep. I was just sort of drifting. You know, that sort of twilight sleep where you're not really awake, but you're not asleep. It's okay. Really. It's just that I've had some strange dreams."

She rolled over on her side, propping herself up on her elbow, suddenly aware that he was in her bed. Well, *on* her bed. Next to her. And despite how he'd startled her, she liked the nearness of him. To make sure it wasn't a dream, she reached out and touched his arm.

It was warm and solid and strong. And he didn't pull away.

"Yeah, I'm having the same kind of night. Except for the not-really-awake part. I've been wide awake the whole time."

He turned over his arm and suddenly her palm was in his. He caressed the top of her hand with his thumb.

"For any particular reason?" she murmured, reining in her mind to keep from imagining that this was going any further than where they were right now. In bed. Together. Touching…

Now, that was a loaded question, Shane thought as he mulled over the many ways he could answer her. Saying he wanted to watch her sleep sounded creepy and it wasn't really the truth. True, he did want to make sure she was safe. Truer still, he'd regretted sending her to bed alone after the good-night kiss they'd shared. He hadn't come in to watch her sleep. He'd come in here hoping to find her just like this, awake and receptive to his touch.

Rather than answer her with words, he lowered his body, stretching out along side of her, propping his head on his free hand. All the while, he didn't let go of her hand.

She went very still for a moment and then she rolled over, so that her lips were a whisper away. Her curves were flush to his body curve for curve—thigh to thigh, abdomen to abdomen, chest to chest.

"I can't sleep when I have unfinished business," she said.

He closed the distance between them, allowing no room for common sense, claiming her lips with his. She responded by moving her hips so that they were square to his, which released all the want and longing that had been bottling up since the day he'd first laid eyes on her. He groaned at the heat that coursed between them, savoring the feel of her, reveling in the anticipation of what was about to happen.

It had been such a long time since he'd felt this way about a woman, since he'd allowed himself to lose control, to go a little crazy.

It was good that they'd had that talk tonight. Even though their future wasn't completely clear, one thing he'd realized since meeting AJ was that the future wasn't a given, that you had to seize every opportunity to live. Right here, right now, he intended to make love to her like this was their last night on earth.

His hand found the hem of her nightgown. It was pushed up around her midriff, and he trailed his finger under the elastic of her panties until he found the curve of her waist. Then he traced his way across the flat expanse of her stomach. She inhaled sharply and her eyes widened.

"Evidently, this isn't a dream." Her voice was softly hoarse in the darkness.

"Well, in some ways it is." He smiled down at her, and brushed a strand of hair off her forehead. "Are you sure about this?"

She nodded, then kissed him lightly on the mouth.

"I wish I could offer you more. I wish I could promise you I'd stay and that we could have a life together here—" Shane kissed her collar bone. Then the dimple at the base of her neck. Then he found her lips. "I want you so badly, I can't think of anything else. So, if right now is enough for you, then—"

"Shh..." She pressed her finger to his lips. "I know you can't promise me anything long term, at least not here. But we have right now. So right now, just kiss me. Make love to me. Let's worry about tomorrow...tomorrow. Because tonight, I'm really glad we're here."

He kissed her softly, then he slowly pushed up her nightgown and pulled it over her head. She was beautiful, all curves and smooth skin. He marveled as he cupped one of her breasts lightly. Dipping his head in reverence, his lips found her neck. He trailed kisses until his mouth closed over a nipple.

The sound of her sighed pleasure made him want her all the more.

He pulled away only so he could roll her over on to her back. He stretched out on top of her, gently nudging her legs apart with his knee. Through his clothes and the thin layer of her panties, he could feel how their bodies would join together perfectly—

But then he felt her stiffen. She bit her lip and looked at him like there was something she needed to say, but couldn't find the words.

Had she changed her mind?

"What's wrong?" he asked, smoothing his hands up her back.

She bit her bottom lip. "It's been a long time since I've… I haven't been with anyone since… So, I'm not on birth control."

He bit back a curse. How could he have been so damn dense? He'd always been careful. He'd never had unprotected sex. It was a chance he wouldn't take for so many different reasons. Yet, tonight he'd pushed toward this union without thinking things through. Mainly because he hadn't been so presumptuous to think that he'd find himself in AJ's bed.

"Well… Wow." He pulled himself off of her, shifted back so he could looked at her. Maybe if they had some space, some room, they could cool off. "I don't have anything, either."

Damn.

Damn.

Damn damn damn damn. He cursed inwardly, because he wanted her so much it almost caused him physical pain. He hoped it didn't show on his face as he stared into her beautiful, tormented blue eyes, hoping to find an answer.

She crossed her arms over her breasts and he realized he'd probably never seen her look so beautiful. That's when he knew… Being here with her like this… Holding her, feeling the warmth of her against him was perfect.

"We don't have to have sex tonight. We can do other things. I'll pick up some condoms tomorrow."

"Umm…well…no…actually, I have condoms." She spat out the words before she lost her nerve. "My friends gave them to me as a…"

As a what? A joke? An incentive?

She was an adult. She didn't need to justify the fact that she was in possession of a box of condoms. It simply meant she practiced safe sex.

Well, she would if she actually had sex. Like she was going to now. Okay, now *she* was blushing. "So, yes, I have condoms. They're in the medicine cabinet in the bathroom. Will you go get them…please?"

He seemed uncertain at first. For a moment she thought he might say no. But then he moved closer and his lips softly brushed hers as he lifted himself off the bed.

When he returned, he took one out of the box and put it on the night stand before he settled in next to her. "I like your friends. They sure know how to give the perfect gift. Tell them I said thanks, okay?" He winked at her, and she reached up and ran her fingers over his jaw line.

She smiled. "So kiss me?"

He complied. They kissed her for a long time. Languid and unhurried kisses that had her convinced, once again, that maybe they were going to take things slow. Considering how that meant she'd still get to touch him, that might be okay. With one stipulation: she tugged at his T-shirt, which had already come untucked from the waistband of his jeans. She pushed it up and he helped her by drawing it over his head.

What had been hidden underneath was pretty close to perfection. She drank in the raw beauty of him, running both hands over his muscles. His biceps were well defined, and his shoulders were broad and ropy, making his torso appear to taper into a graceful V that disappeared beneath the waistband of his jeans. It made her wonder about other parts of him that were out of sight.

She inhaled sharply.

Pace yourself.

She steadied herself by allowing her hands to travel over his abs, memorizing his form and the feel of the muscles under her hands.

She was so caught up in the beauty and feel of him, of his skin on her skin, that she was a little startled when he slid her panties down and his hand glided over her hips, down to her thighs and dipped between them.

This was really going to happen. She was ready and hyper-aware of every breath, every kiss, every touch. When his hand found her centermost heat, she shivered with erotic ecstasy. She noticed that his whole body trembled, too. As his hips surged, searching for her innermost harbor, she welcomed him by opening her thighs so that their bodies could be even closer.

"Shane," she whispered. "Oh…Shane…"

The rest of what she said was lost in his kiss. He touched her with such care, and seemed to instinctively know exactly what made her feel good.

She wanted to him to feel good, too. She needed to touch him, to give him even a fraction of the pleasure he was giving her. So she slid her hand between their bodies, reaching for his hips. But he grabbed her wrist and held her hand away from his arousal.

"Not yet."

"Why not?"

"Just…not yet." His rapt breathlessness stole her own breath. "When you touch me, you make me… crazy. And this…this time is for you."

His lips reclaimed hers. He released her hand and found her hot center again. The more he touched her and kissed her, the more aroused they both became.

The way he touched her proved exactly how much he wanted her…but his hunger for her was never so evident as when he came up for air and devoured her with reverent, voracious eyes.

She couldn't get enough of the way he touched her. As if he read her mind, his touch demanded more. Still gentle, but more forcefully, he drove into her with such intensity she fisted her hands in to his hair and gasped, arching against him. She was enraptured by him, by the pulsing heat that was growing and throbbing in her.

"Let yourself go," he whispered in her ear, his voice a husky rasp. "Just let go, AJ."

Maybe it was the heat of his voice in her ear, more likely it was the way he virtually made her levitate with his magic touch, but a moment later she went over the edge. He held her, until she rode out the wave.

She curled into his body and buried her face in his chest, needing to get as close to him as she could. He enfolded her in his arms and held her tight. She lost herself again in the fortress of his broad shoulders, the smoothness and warmth of his skin.

"How was that?" His voice was a hoarse and throaty rasp.

When she lifted her head and looked at him, his eyes searched her face.

"It was great. Really, fabulously great."

He smiled. "And that was just the warm up."

Snuggling into him, she could feel his erection pressing into her leg. "Well, then, I'm prepared to have my mind blown."

The thought of his body—so sexy and tight—inside her was enough to make the heat glow in her again. She wanted him more now than before he'd first touched her.

She put a little space between them and unbuttoned his fly. Slowly, she unzipped it and together they got him out of his pants and his underwear. This first glimpse of all of him made her wet and ready. She reached out and brushed her fingertips over him. His body shuddered. He inhaled a sharp breath into his lungs, his head fell back slightly. She devoured his male glory, from his flat, muscled stomach…up farther to his biceps and his shoulders…to his throat and the shadowed, imperfect beauty of his face. She stroked him and learned every inch of him, committing it to memory, but he didn't let her linger for long. He pulled away and she thought she would go over the edge again, as she watched him put the condom on the generous length of his maleness. After he was done, he made his way back to her body, and stretched out on top of her. He settled into the cradle of her hips. The knowledge of what was about to happen made her shudder with excitement. He entered her with a tender, unhurried push.

The heat that radiated from Shane seeped into her. His body was stiff as he gently inched forward, going so very slow and being so careful. As her body adjusted to welcome him, she joined him in a slow, rocking rhythm.

Pleasure began to rise and she angled her hips up to intensify the sensation. His bare skin against hers was a breathtaking pleasure that was almost too much to for her to handle.

She was so aware of him, of the two of them fused so close that it seemed they were joined body and soul.

Their union seemed so very right she cried out

from the sheer pleasure of it. Shane let go of her hands, moaned and then buried his head in the curve of her neck.

She eased her palms down his back, wondering about his life, wondering about the time he'd spent in different parts of the world, wondering about the woman in Italy he was still so hung up on… Even though she only knew a few things about his life, she sensed she knew his heart very well.

The thought made her kiss him hard and fast, and then things got a little crazy as she wrapped her legs around his waist and dug her nails into his shoulders. He didn't seem to mind how tightly she was clinging to him. So she held him in place by the shoulders and shifted under him. The way he groaned was so delicious that she arched beneath him again and drew him deeper inside.

At that moment, staring down into her clear eyes, his body joined with hers, Shane felt the mantle of his life shift. All of a sudden, without explanation, his world was different.

Oh, no, he thought. It wasn't possible?

But it was. He was in love with her smile and her mind and the way she felt in his arms right now. It was the smoothness of her skin and the way she smelled and the way she gazed up at him with a look in her eyes that seemed to mirror his very own feelings. It was everything he knew about her and all the things he had yet to discover about her. And, yeah, though it made him a total caveman, but the fact that he was the first man in five years to make love to her nearly knocked him out.

"Shane?" Her eyes searched his face. "Are you… okay?"

"I am absolutely better than okay." He kissed her deeply, pulling her to him so tightly that every inch of their bodies were fully joined. Then he gathered her in his arms and held her tight. He hadn't particularly cared how close he'd felt to other women he'd been intimate with. But as he built up to the pace that would transport AJ and him to Nirvana, he wanted to see her face. He needed a one hundred percent connection. Not just body to body, but eye to eye and soul to soul.

It didn't take long before their bond, coupled with the rhythmic motion of their bodies carried them over the edge. As he lay with her, sweaty and spent, he cradled her against him.

As he'd made love to her, three words had been racing around his head. Now they'd somehow found their way to the tip of his tongue.

Oh, man... Don't do that, he thought. *You're caught up in the moment. Don't say things you don't mean.*

The problem was, he did mean it. With all his soul.

Even so, him meaning it and following through with the implications of "I love you" were two very different things.

* * *

She looked up at him. “Are you okay?”

He wanted to tell her exactly how he felt, how she made him feel. Except when he opened his mouth all that came out was, “I couldn’t be better.”

Maybe it was the words that were bottled up inside, but something had his eyes stinging a little. He didn’t want her to think he was disappointed in her. That was so not the case. He was disappointed in himself, in the situation that put a barrier between them. So, instead of ruining the moment, he snuggled closer to her, and tried to live in the present. Not in the not-so-distant future when they would have to say goodbye.

Chapter Twelve

Shane parked his truck on the cobblestone circular driveway in front of Agnes Sherwood's mansion. He slanted a glance at AJ, who was sitting beside him.

"Who all is going to be here tonight?" he asked.

"Just my grandmother and my mother. So, you'll get to meet her."

Earlier that day, Agnes had summoned AJ and him to dinner at her home that evening. Interesting that a woman who prided herself on being the poster child of propriety would issue a last-minute invite for which they'd made themselves available because it wasn't so much an invitation as a summons.

"What's your mom like?"

"We look a lot alike, actually. As far as her demeanor, she's one of the sweetest women you'll ever meet. She's bent over backward trying to get back into Grandmother's good graces. I think I told you that my grandmother basically disowned her when she married my father. Then, as she started having kids, my grandmother realized that by cutting her daughter out of her life, she was also cutting out her grandkids. So my grandmother opened the lines of communication…slightly. But it wasn't until after my father died that Grandmother played the martyr and really allowed the lines of communication to reopen. But it was strictly on Grandmother's terms. That's how it's always been. It was totally ridiculous, because my mother could've had the upper hand with my grandmother because she controlled when she got to see the grandkids. But in my mother's eyes, it would've been punishing *us* to keep us from our grandmother." AJ shook her head. "As far as I'm concerned, nobody has any business dictating anyone's life. As you can see, my mother does not hold the same opinion. My grandmother pushes her around all the time. For example, when I was fourteen and it came time to ship me off to Le Claire, my mom practically packed my bags for me because she knew my studying at Le Claire was exactly what my grandmother wanted. And, of course, since Grandmother footed the bill, whatever Grandmother wanted, Grandmother got. She still does for the most part. I'm her biggest disappointment because I'm the nonconformist of the family. All my sisters went to an Ivy League school because our grandmother had the power to get us in. But I opted out and chose culinary school. Big disappointment."

She said it with a shrug and expression that indicated she wasn't ashamed. Shane nodded, unsure of how he was supposed to respond to this. Things were better than ever between them since last night, and he intended to keep it on a good course.

Hopefully, that would help AJ make up her mind about Italy.

"I certainly didn't want to sound like I'm slamming my family," AJ continued. "I suppose my mother is a better woman than I am because she's so wonderfully sweet. She just can't say no to my grandmother. Yet the problem between them lingers. It's certainly not for lack of effort on Mom's part. But that's a big enough Sherwood-Antonelli baggage dump for one evening. Come in and see the show for yourself."

"That's quite an introduction," Shane said.

"It's not too late to back out," AJ said with a gleam in her eye.

Shane leaned in a kissed her soundly on the lips. "Let's go in. The sooner we get there the sooner we can go home. Not that I don't want to spend time with your family. It's just that's I've been looking forward to getting you alone since I left for work this morning."

Shane got out and walked around the truck and opened AJ's door. She stood so close they were nearly toe to toe. He wanted to gather her in his arms. Probably not the thing to do in Agnes Sherwood's driveway.

AJ straightened his tie and picked a piece of lint off his collar. Mrs. Sherwood didn't seem to like him very much. So, he had no idea why she'd invited him tonight. He did his best to project a demeanor of calm and collected, but on the inside he felt as if he were walking into enemy territory—or at best, a lion's den.

It turned out that Grandmother had called the dinner party to thank Shane for all he'd done to "support Agnes Jane through this unfortunate time."

Since that was totally out of character, AJ had to believe she had an ulterior motive. She wanted to check out this man her granddaughter was spending so much time with. She was testing his mettle. Why she would bother was a mystery to AJ—other than maybe the old woman was still trying to win this battle of wills with her granddaughter.

The cocktail hour went better than AJ had hoped. Shane had one of those personalities that ebbed and flowed with the tide. He was charming and engaging with AJ's mother, Rebecca. He politely held his own with Agnes, putting in plugs for AJ's culinary talents every chance he got, to which her grandmother would throw out a barb such as, "cooking is something the hired help does."

AJ had vowed she would not be goaded into an argument tonight. That's why she was surprised when it wasn't her grandmother that she wanted to exchange words with. It was Shane, of all people. He announced to her mother and grandmother that he was trying to convince her to come to Italy with him.

AJ nearly choked on her drink. Her mother made polite noises, but didn't really say anything. Grandmother sat there like a queen on her throne wearing her normal I-smell-something-and-it-doesn't-smell-good expression.

"Think about it," he said, obviously determined to sell the idea. "Since she is without a kitchen and office for the time being, she could come to Italy while it's being rebuilt. I will be able to retire in less than a year. And then we will see where that leaves us. It makes perfect sense to me."

AJ stood. "I will have a kitchen and office—even if they're temporary—before I cater the Lapham wedding. Then it will be business as usual. So, I can't go because I will lose more business."

Agnes finally broke the silence, "Are you suggesting you want to marry my granddaughter?"

A croaking noise escaped before AJ could stifle it. Still, she was able to get out the words, "Shane, why don't you come with me and I'll give you a tour of the house and the garden?"

Before he had a chance to answer, AJ had herded him off toward the back of the house.

"What are you doing?" she asked. "Why did you tell them about Italy?"

Shane smiled a devilish smile. "I figured if your

grandmother is so against you cooking, she might be an ally and help the cause. But…I'm surprised. You didn't let me answer her question. The one about whether I wanted to marry you."

A ringing sound akin to the symphony of cicadas that performed nightly outside AJ's bedroom window started in her ears. She felt a flush begin in her cleavage and spread upward. "Don't tease about things like that, okay?"

AJ yanked on his arm.

"Come here. I want you to see something." She took him by the hand and led him to the kitchen at the back of the house.

"Look at this," she finally said.

A catering company was plating the salad and preparing the dinner.

"She hired one of my competitors for tonight. There are so many catering companies in the Dallas area that if I take off even a few months I will have to start over at square one. I will lose all the momentum I'm gaining by landing the Lapham wedding."

"In your grandmother's defense, wouldn't it have been a bit difficult for you to cater tonight *and* attend the party?" Shane asked.

"Party? What party? Honestly, I'd be more comfortable in the kitchen—in this kitchen—" she gestured around the cavernous room "—cooking than I am sitting out there sipping champagne cocktails waiting to be called to the table. I mean, *look* at this kitchen. Do you know what I'd give to have access to it? And to think Grandmother never sets foot in here. Shane, I can't come with you. Don't you see? I just can't, so please don't ask me again."

Chapter Thirteen

"Oh, my gosh! Are you crazy?" Pepper shrieked. "You could write a cookbook while you were over in Europe. Think of all the new recipes you'd come home with. And the shoes. And you might even come home engaged."

Ahh, there was the real reason.

AJ should've known better than to confide in her friends about Shane's pseudo-proposal and his invitation to Italy. As they gathered for their weekly brunch at AJ's house, her girlfriends were on it like white on rice, insisting that she was crazy not to go.

"I can't, guys. I'd have to close up shop."

"In my professional opinion, I think it would be quite good for business. You'd come back having all this European experience. People would eat that up, if you'll pardon the pun."

The three laughed. Then Pepper nudged Sydney and the three exchanged a certain look. Why was it that lately she always felt like the only one left out of the inside joke?

"Well, funny you should mention closing up," said Sydney. "Because I just might be looking for a job soon. I was hoping that Celebrations might be in need of a front-of-the-house person."

"What? What's going on at work?" AJ pushed aside her curried-chicken salad and trained her full, serious attention on Sydney.

Sydney told them about how each department head had been given boxes of documents to shred, and how, for the third time this year, they'd switched the figures for the quarterly earnings statement at the last minute before publishing. She didn't know whether the figures were correct or not, but she had suspicions that they weren't. Now she feared the answers she needed were in the reams of paper that staff had worked around the clock to destroy.

"Something isn't right," Sydney said. "And I'm not sure if I'm helping them do something illegal by publishing false numbers and destroying corporate documents."

AJ looked at Pepper to gage her reaction. All Pepper did was shrug. "I don't know. I asked Daddy if everything was okay and he truly acted like he had no clue what I was talking about. You know, he and

Mama have spent several months of this year out of the country. I can't imagine he'd be out of the loop, but I can't imagine him being so nonchalant if something was up and I, of all people, was asking questions. Because that would mean word was getting out and I think he'd freak."

"Or maybe he's smart enough to put two and two together," Sydney said. "And he realizes we're friends and I told you everything I know. That's why I have to get out of there."

"So, you see," said Caroline. "It's looking very auspicious for you to go to Italy. Caroline can hold down the fort and you can go with Shane and fortify the business by your European connection."

"There's only one problem," AJ said, their persistence and overcoming of her objections was starting to make her squirm.

"And that would be?" asked Caroline.

"Syd and Pepper are brilliant when it comes to bookings and front of the house, and you've already earned yourself the title of Pastry Goddess, but one detail you're forgetting is the savory kitchen. That's the majority of our business. If I go, Celebrations will be left without a chef."

They exchanged that look again and it was starting to get on her nerves. Obviously they'd been having discussions without her.

"Hear me out," said Pepper. "We all know you're irreplaceable, but the menu is small and you've been working hard on honing the right recipes. What would happen if you trained a chef to work in your absence? He or she could follow your recipes and anything new would have to pass the three-way test." She motioned to herself, Caroline and Sydney.

The gesture almost looked like she was making the sign of the cross.

"We know Celebrations, Inc. I mean, you've used us to perfect the items you're offering now."

Pepper reached out and put her hand on AJ's. "For months you've been after us to officially come on board. Now is our chance."

AJ gulped. The woman knew how to play hard ball. She was pushing all the right buttons.

"Let me ask you something," said Sydney. "Do you love him?"

Yes.

Her heart screamed the answer, but for some reason, she couldn't form the word on her lips and put the declaration out into the universe.

Maybe it was the fact that Italy held so many bad memories for Shane. Bad memories and bad luck. It scared her to death. She didn't want to be painted into that bad-mojo motif, not to mention that she didn't want to move to a foreign country if he still had unfinished business with this Manuela woman.

A woman he'd met when he was a teenager and hadn't had contact with since. It was, she had to admit, unlikely she would come between them.

And, of course, she just might be the person—or

this might be the time—that Italy and Shane got on better terms.

She couldn't be sure.

For that matter, she knew from experience that life carried no guarantees.

So then, what she so afraid of?

As luck would have it, at that moment her telephone rang. Seizing the opportunity to escape, AJ hopped up and answered it.

"*Bonjour,* AJ! It's Maya. How are you?"

A shiver—a good shiver, but a shiver nonetheless because of the sheer coincidence of the timing—shimmied down her spine.

It was Maya, her friend from St. Michel, proprietress of Maya's Chocolates, which were rumored to make people fall in love. Maya—the one who had landed Shane on her doorstep bearing a gift of her chocolates sent special delivery from Maya herself—managing to ring the phone just as AJ was having trouble making the decision that could possibly change the course of her life forever.

As if Maya had reached through the phone line and given her that final nudge, AJ's heart swelled and took the metaphorical tumble she'd been so vigilantly guarding against.

Suddenly, she knew exactly what she had to do.

AJ planned a special dinner.

Pepper and Sydney came over and erected a small gauzy canopy, strung it with lights and candles, turning it into something that looked like a magical fairy land. A *romantic,* magical fairy land.

After all, they had a lot to celebrate and she couldn't wait to tell him the good news—that she'd managed to arrange everything so she could go to Italy with him when he left next month.

But she wanted to save the news for dessert, if she could. It would be hard to keep it to herself until then, but she'd try. Or maybe she'd meet him at the door with a flute of bubbly and a huge, deep kiss and then she would tell him.

The champagne was chilled and AJ was in the process of carrying the hors d'oeuvres outside when there was a knock on the door.

He was early.

Funny, though, why would he knock rather than letting himself in?

Quickly, she grabbed a champagne glass and filled it as much as she could before it bubbled over.

Should she take two glasses so that they could have a toast? No, too formal, and she'd probably end up spilling both glasses in the process of trying to hand him one and hug him.

So she opted for one and quickly made her way to the door. When she opened it, it was not Shane standing there, but the sheriff, looking pale and grim.

"AJ, I'm sorry to come to your door bearing bad news, but there's been an accident."

AJ nearly dropped the flute as she steadied herself by gripping the door. "Shane?"

She heard herself utter his name, but it sounded as if it came from somewhere else.

The sheriff nodded.

"What happened?"

"We don't know the entire situation, but from what we can piece together so far, it looks like somebody messed with his tires and one of them blew. He lost control and the truck flipped."

Hearing those words, the glass slipped from AJ's hand and smashed on the floor. This couldn't be happening.

As the sheriff took her arm and helped her over to the couch to sit down, nightmares of the evening she heard the news about Danny flooded back. It was like an ugly instant reply. A Pandora's box of never-ending bad news.

How could this be happening again? She'd given her heart to a man, only to have him taken away.

She took a deep breath, bracing herself for the answer to the question she had to ask.

"Is he…alive?"

Chapter Fourteen

Shane opened his eyes and blinked at the strange surroundings. He winced at the blinding pain that shot through his head. For a moment, he didn't know where he was or how he had gotten there. Then, in a flash and rush, his memory returned.

He'd gone home to shower, change clothes and get Houdini before he headed over to AJ's house for dinner. She'd said she had something exciting to tell him and he was in a hurry to get there. That was the last thing he remembered.

He must've been in an accident.

Houdini had been in the car. *Dammit, where is he?*

Shane found the nurse call button and pressed it several times.

The doctor was actually the one who answered the call. The sheriff was trailing in behind him.

Shane tried to sit up, but the pain made him fall back. Now he realized that not only did his head hurt, but the pain extended all the way down his body to his toes.

"What the hell happened to me?" he asked.

"Your truck flipped. They believe someone tampered with your tires and one of them blew when you were driving. You flipped your car and sustained a concussion, some broken ribs and a broken femur. You're pretty banged up, but you're going to be okay. The sheriff needs to talk to you to get a report. Do you feel up to it?"

Shane scrubbed his hand over his face then looked at the cop. "Sure, but first—my dog was in the truck with me. Is he okay?"

"Yes, he's fine. The airbag cushioned the impact. Don't worry, he's over at your girlfriend's house. She specifically wanted us to make sure you know that your dog is fine and she is taking good care of him."

AJ. Oh, God.

"How long have I been here?"

"About forty-eight hours," the doctor said. "We've had to keep you sedated to manage the pain. That leg of yours was in pretty bad shape. We had to set the fracture. You're lucky if you don't remember."

He didn't, and he said a silent prayer of thanks—for that and because Houdini was okay. He'd gotten attached to that damn dog, whether he wanted to admit it or not. He was glad the mutt was okay. AJ must've been out of her mind when she heard.

"When can I see my girlfriend?" he asked.

"Right after you finish with the sheriff. She was here for the better part of the day. She just stepped out about fifteen minutes ago. But she asked us to call her if you woke up while she was gone."

"Would you please call her?" Shane asked. "Maybe she'll get here as we're finishing up."

"I'll have one of the nurses do that right now."

"By the way, Doc, did anyone contact my commanding officer? If not, they must think I've gone AWOL."

"I'll check your chart to see who they spoke with, but someone in military dress was here checking on you yesterday."

In the meantime, the sheriff grilled him about whether or not he'd seen anyone suspicious loitering in the parking lot.

"It's a rent-by-the-week apartment. A lot of people come and go. But I didn't see anyone or anything out of the ordinary."

By the time the sheriff finished his questioning, Shane felt like he hadn't been a tremendous help.

"So, what makes you think this was intentional as opposed to a random tire blowout?"

The sheriff took his time folding up his small notebook and putting it back in his breast pocket.

"Well, for one thing, the three tires that are still intact had been slashed. Not badly enough to flatten them, just enough to where the right kind of friction might cause them to blow. Somebody knew what they were doing."

"Oh, hell," Shane muttered under his breath. What if AJ had been in the truck with him when this happened? But she wasn't, thank God. Something else to be grateful for. And he was sure he'd really begin to feel the gratitude once his body quit throbbing.

As the sheriff left, Shane pressed the nurse call button and asked if he could have something for the pain. A moment later, AJ walked in.

"Hi," AJ said as she approached his bedside. "How are you feeling?"

He tried to smile. "Honestly, I've felt better physically. But now that you're here, I know I'm going to be okay."

He winked at her.

"Always the charmer." She smiled even though her eyes looked sad, like she'd been crying.

"Hey, don't worry," he said. "Everything's going to be okay. Do you hear me?"

She nodded.

"So, how's that dog of mine? Has he been minding his manners?"

"Of course he has. He misses you. Asked me to tell you hello."

At least her sense of humor was coming back.

"So he's talking now, huh? Wonders never cease. And speaking of talking, the last time I talked to you, you said you had something exciting to tell me. What is it?"

Her sad eyes searched his face for a moment. She didn't look very happy for someone who'd been sitting on good news for a couple of days.

"Oh, it was nothing, really." She waved away the question as if the answer were trivial.

"No, tell me. I could use some cheering up."

Again, she hesitated. "It's not important. I was just excited about you coming over for dinner. There really wasn't any news. At least nothing that matters now."

Then a nurse who was brandishing a syringe of painkiller entered the room. "Okay, hon, you ready for this? It'll only sting for a moment and then it'll knock you out. So, you better say good-night to your girl because you're not going to be very good company after I get through with you."

"What do you mean you've changed your mind?" Sydney asked, dumbfounded. "How can you pass up a chance to live in Italy?"

Her proper British accent reminded AJ that Sydney had, in fact, lived over there and knew the European sensibility. To her it was an outrage that a person would pass up such an opportunity.

For that matter, Caroline and Pepper were uncharacteristically quiet. Pepper paced back and forth in AJ's kitchen, where they were meeting to go over the specifics for the Lapham wedding—and trying to come up with an alternate plan if they weren't able to find a commercial kitchen within a reasonable distance.

"AJ," she wailed. "I think we need to have an intervention here before you lose the love of your life. Why is it that everyone can see this but you?"

What was there to say to that? The conclusion she'd come to was avoiding the pain of losing love was more important than the pleasure of being in love.

No. That didn't sound right. Didn't feel right, either. But it was too much to deal with right now. The Lapham wedding was a week away, and she still didn't have a kitchen.

A pang of sadness nearly pierced her heart. She wasn't sure if it was because that really wasn't her philosophy, or at least she didn't want it to be. Or because she didn't want to hurt Shane while he was already in such physical pain. But she couldn't take the chance of opening herself up for the hurt of losing yet another man.

"You guys, I confided in you because I trust you. You have to promise me that you will not talk about this to anyone else—at least not until I have a chance to tell Shane myself."

The only good part was at least she hadn't told him that she'd very briefly considered going with him. At least it would only involve a slow and gradual distancing that would happen naturally as it drew closer to the day he left Celebration and she wasn't going with him.

"Why, though?" Caroline asked. "Why are you doing this?"

AJ tool a deep breath, cleared her throat as she thought about the best way to explain it.

"I guess Shane's accident really drove home the point that Shane and Danny are a lot more alike than I realized."

"How do you figure that?" asked Caroline. "And if it's true, why is it such a bad thing? You loved Danny. You love Shane. So…?"

"Well, starting with the fact that both of their jobs are dangerous and put them in harm's way. I mean, sure, at the moment, Shane is pushing pencils and paper as he oversees the renovation of that building, but even he said that his assignment could change at a moment's notice."

Her friends stared at her as if issuing a silent, *And?*

"What if I got over to Italy and he got transferred somewhere else? Like a war zone. Or worse yet, what if his assignment had to do with counterterrorism? That's his specialty after all, and it wouldn't be such a stretch for the army to utilize his strengths to the fullest before they let him retire."

"But you don't know this. There's a bigger possibility that none of this will happen."

AJ shook her head. "I can't bear the thought of losing another love in the line of duty, especially when that duty might take us so far away from home."

There. Even as irrational as it might have sounded, she'd said it, and the phone rang, as if punctuating her declaration.

"Hello?" she said into the receiver.

"Agnes Jane, I've been trying to reach you for days," said Grandmother. "Why haven't you called me back?"

AJ loosened her jaw as soon as she realized she was gritting her teeth. Great, only seconds into the conversation and she was already tense.

"I'm sorry, *Grandmother,*" she emphasized the word so her friends would understand who she was talking to. If they were indeed good friends after she'd hung up from this phone call they'd call off the so-called intervention, as they called it.

A girl could only stand so much combat in a single day.

"I've had a few things on my mind. I don't know if you heard, but Shane was in an accident and he's been in the hospital. So while I've been visiting him, I've silenced my phone. But how may I help you?"

"Yes, I was sorry to hear about his accident." AJ was surprised that her grandmother's voice actually held notes of compassion. She wasn't sure she'd ever heard that tone before. It sort of freaked her out a little. But, then again, in her own way, Agnes always did seem to have a soft spot for Shane. Or maybe a not-as-hard spot was a better way to describe it.

She guessed it should be points in Shane's favor that her grandmother didn't hate him in the way she'd hated the other men who had come and gone in the lives of her mother and sisters.

"I've also been running around like crazy trying to secure a commercial kitchen that I can use for the Lapham wedding. That's next week, you know."

"Of course I know. I'm attending." The hard edge was back in Agnes's voice, and AJ felt her own jaw tightening again. "And the reason I've been trying to get in touch with you is to offer you the use of my kitchen."

AJ straightened and glanced at her friends, as if they, too, could hear what Agnes had just said. But of course, they couldn't, and that left them waving to get her attention and mouthing *What? What's going on?*

AJ turned her back on them because she couldn't answer now. Now, she wasn't sure she'd heard what she thought she had.

Cautiously, she asked, "What exactly do you mean?"

The question was generic enough that if she had misunderstood, her grandmother was sure to clarify.

"What do I mean? What else would I mean? I am allowing you to bring the food you intend to cook for the wedding over to my home and you may use my kitchen to prepare it. I'm also willing to lend you the services of my chef, if you're shorthanded."

AJ could hardly believe what she was hearing.

Despite the sharp edge to her grandmother's voice, she was being...*helpful?* Whoa, wait, something must be off-kilter or there must be a catch. Agnes Sherwood did not want AJ to succeed at being a chef. In fact, AJ had always sensed that the older woman had been waiting in the wings just waiting for the day she could pronounce AJ and her silly catering dreams a colossal failure.

Normally, AJ would be grateful having received such an offer, but this was her grandmother after all. All indicators demanded AJ proceed with caution.

"Why?" she asked. Okay, she could've couched the question in a more polite manner. But she had so much on her mind, with the wedding, and Shane being injured and her friends giving her a hard time about a decision that had been extremely hard to make.

"What do you mean *why?* Agnes Jane, don't be so crass. When someone is doing you a favor it's good form to simply say 'thank you.'"

Okay, not today, Grandmother. AJ just didn't have it in her to play the "appease Agnes Sherwood" game.

"No, I have every reason to ask you *why.* You have wanted me to fail since the day you learned I wanted to go to culinary school rather than the university you'd picked out for me. I'll tell you what, I am not going to fail. You might as well get used to that right now. I'm not like my sisters and my mother—no offense to them, or to you for that matter—but I don't need your help, especially if it comes with strings attached or a strategically placed banana peel for me to slip on."

Agnes was silent on the other end of the line. So silent that for a moment AJ thought she might have hung up on her, which wouldn't have been surprising.

"Why would I want you to fail at this job? Frances Lapham is a good friend. How do you think you got the job? I told her to hire you."

The slap of the backhanded admission stunned AJ for a moment. Was this an endorsement from her grandmother, or a statement that AJ wouldn't have landed the Lapham wedding on her own?

"Of course, Frances insisted on the tasting, which you pulled off with flying colors. That's why she contracted you, because apparently you did such a beautiful job with everything. She said everything was exquisite. She told me you have a real gift when it comes to food. Not that I needed her to help me see that."

Once again, AJ was stunned silent. But only for a few seconds. "I don't know what to say, Grandmother. Other than thank you. For believing in me. And for the use of your kitchen."

"Of course I believe in you, Agnes Jane. You're my namesake and the only one of my granddaughters who is strong enough to stand on her own two feet. It's taken a while for you to prove yourself to me, but now I know. I see it in the business you've built on your own. I see it in the way you stand up for yourself. I even see it in that young man you're dating."

Ooh. Oh, no. *Was* dating. The words made that pain her heart stab again. But AJ and her friends were the only ones who knew this. At least for right now. Because she would continue to take care of Shane and Houdini, until Shane was able to care for himself.

"You know, he's the one who asked me to let you use the kitchen. Pretty sharp guy. He has my seal of approval. Not that you've ever needed my approval. I never thought I'd admit this to you, but I've always admired that in you, too. You have a good head on your shoulders, Agnes Jane. Of all my children and grandchildren, you're the one who makes sound decisions. I don't have to worry about you."

When Shane opened his eyes, AJ's beautiful face was the first thing that came into focus. Just seeing her there made him feel as if her were…home.

She smoothed his hair and softly trailed the back of her hand across his cheek. He turned his head so he could kiss her hand.

"I'm so glad you're here," he said. "I have so much to tell you."

"Me, too," she said, looking a little anxious.

"The sheriff came by today and said they finally arrested that group of boys who have been causing so much trouble. He said even though they couldn't pin the tire slashing and accident on them, some of the fingerprints matched. But they're holding them over at the county jail on charges of breaking and entering. They got the whole lot of them.

AJ's hands flew to her mouth, a gesture of relief and surprise. He couldn't wait to see her reaction when he told her the other piece of news. But—

"Okay, now you tell me your news," he said.

The relief he'd witnessed before was gone, something deeper, more resolute shone in her eyes.

"Remember the other day when you asked about my exciting news? Well, I'm ready to share it now. Shane, I want to move to Italy with you. I'll admit at first I was scared. After your accident, I'd even talked myself out of going with you. It was because I was scared. Scared of leaving Celebration, but as it turns out, I'm more afraid of losing you than I am of losing it. Celebration will always be here. I need to be with you."

She exhaled like she'd gotten a load of weight off her chest. Shane was elated, but also a little concerned about how his other piece of news would sit with her.

"Wow. I'm so glad that you want to go with me. I just hope that what I'm going to tell you doesn't change the way you feel."

She paled a little and he took her hand, kissed her knuckles.

"I got another piece of important news today. Now, you'll have to help me figure out what we're going to do." He looked into her eyes for a moment before he continued. "Lying in a hospital bed day in and day out gives a guy a lot of time to think. And overthink things, as the case may be. I was beginning to get the feeling that you weren't very thrilled about going to Italy. Well, I decided that if you weren't going, I wasn't going, either. I don't need Italy anymore."

He paused, wanting his words to sink in. He could tell by her expression that she understood the magnitude of what he was saying: he didn't need to go to Italy to get closure with his family. What he needed was a family of his own. He'd found that right here in Celebration. For twenty years he'd been thinking—whether he realized it or not—that he might someday make a life with Manuela. But over the course of twenty years, Manuela had become more fiction than real life because with her he could write his own story. And it was always in his head. No real life woman could measure up to the fictional Manuela who lived in his mind.

Until he met AJ and learned the real meaning of living.

"This broken leg changes the entire dynamic of everything," he said. "Since the fracture was so severe, I'm going to need several months of recovery time. That won't be very conducive to traveling or moving.

"So when my commanding officer came in to check on me a couple of days ago, I asked about the possibility of finishing out my active duty time before I retire here, in Celebration. We don't have to move if you don't want to, AJ. I know your family is here and your business is here. Houdini is here. What would we do with him if we moved?"

He couldn't remember ever seeing AJ look this happy. The tears that shimmered in her eyes made them look even bluer than the European oceans he used to swim in as a teen. It dawned on him that maybe all those years he'd been swimming those waters, he'd been searching for the woman in front of him now.

"I love you and I want what makes you happy," he said. "Because being with you is all I need to be happy. So what do you say? May I stay here in Celebration with you? We can visit Italy, if you really want to go. Maybe we could even spend our honeymoon there?"

Her sharp intake of breath made him smile. And then her surprise morphed into a smile of sheer delight.

"Why, are you proposing?" she asked.

"Maybe I am," he said. "Wait, scratch that. Yes, I am. I *definitely* am."

* * * * *

COMING NEXT MONTH from Harlequin® Special Edition®

AVAILABLE SEPTEMBER 18, 2012

#2215 THE MAVERICK'S READY-MADE FAMILY

Montana Mavericks: Back in the Saddle

Brenda Harlen

Soon-to-be single mom Antonia Wright isn't looking for romance, single dad Clayton Traub only wants to make a new start with his infant son, and neither one is prepared for the attraction that sizzles between them....

#2216 A HOME FOR NOBODY'S PRINCESS

Royal Babies

Leanne Banks

What happens when a Texas nanny learns she is the biological daughter of a prince? Her rancher boss steps in to help protect her from the paparazzi, but who can protect her from her attraction to him?

#2217 CORNER-OFFICE COURTSHIP

The Camdens of Colorado

Victoria Pade

There's only one thing out of Cade Camden's reach—Nati Morrison, whose family was long ago wronged by his.

#2218 TEXAS MAGIC

Celebrations, Inc.

Nancy Robards Thompson

Caroline Coopersmith simply wanted to make it through the weekend of her bridezilla younger sister's wedding. She never intended on falling in love with best man Drew Montgomery.

#2219 DADDY IN THE MAKING

St. Valentine, Texas

Crystal Green

He'd lost most of his memories, and he was back in town to recover them. But when he met the woman who haunted his dreams, what he recovered was himself.

#2220 THE SOLDIER'S BABY BARGAIN

Home to Harbor Town

Beth Kery

Ryan fell for Faith without ever setting eyes on her. Their first night together exploded in unexpected passion. Now, he must prove not only that the baby she carries is his, but that they belong together.

What happens when a Texas nanny learns she is the biological daughter of a prince? Her rancher boss steps in to help protect her from the paparazzi, but who can protect her from her attraction to him?

Read on for an excerpt of
A HOME FOR NOBODY'S PRINCESS
by USA TODAY *bestselling author Leanne Banks.*

Available October 2012

"This is out of control." Benjamin sighed. "Well, damn. I guess I'm gonna have to be your fiancé."

Coco's jaw dropped. "What?"

"It won't be real," he said quickly, as much for himself as for her. After the debacle of his relationship with Brooke, the idea of an engagement nearly gave him hives. "It's just for the sake of appearances until the insanity dies down. This way it won't look like you're all alone and ready to have someone take advantage of you. If someone approaches you, then they'll have to deal with me, too."

She frowned. "I'm stronger than I seem," she said.

"I know you're strong. After what you went through for your mom and helping Emma to settle down, I know you're strong. But it's gotta be damn tiring to feel like you've always got to be on guard."

Coco sighed and her shoulders slumped. "You're right about that." She met his gaze with a wince. "Are you sure you don't mind doing this?"

"It's just for a little while," he said. "You mentioned that a fiancé would fix things a few minutes ago. I had to run it through my brain. It seems like the right thing to do."

HSEEXP1012

She gave a slow nod and bit her lip. “Hmm. But it would cut into your dating time.”

Benjamin laughed. “That’s not a big focus at the moment.”

“It would be a huge relief for me,” she admitted. “If you’re sure you don’t mind. And we’ll break it off the second you feel inconvenienced.”

“No problem,” he said. “I’ll spread the word. Should be all over the county by lunchtime. No one can know the truth. That’s the only way this will work.”

Coco took a deep breath and closed her eyes as if preparing to take a jump into deep water. “Okay” she said, and opened her eyes. “Let’s do it.”

Will Coco be able to carry out the charade?

Find out in Leanne Banks’s new novel—
A HOME FOR NOBODY’S PRINCESS.

Available October 2012 from Harlequin® Special Edition®

HSEEXP1012

HARLEQUIN
Blaze
red-hot reads

At their grandmother's request, three estranged sisters return home for Christmas to the small town of Beckett's Run. Little do they know that this family reunion will reveal long-buried secrets... and new-found love.

Discover the magic of Christmas in a brand-new Harlequin® Romance miniseries.

In October 2012, find yourself
SNOWBOUND IN THE EARL'S CASTLE
by **Fiona Harper**

Be enchanted in November 2012 by a
SLEIGH RIDE WITH THE RANCHER
by **Donna Alward**

And be mesmerized in December 2012 by
MISTLETOE KISSES WITH THE BILLIONAIRE
by **Shirley Jump**

Available wherever books are sold.

www.Harlequin.com

HR17837